created and
written by
WARREN ELLIS

artwork
MIKE WOLFER

tones
DAN PARSONS

cover color
NIMBUS

editor in chief
WILLIAM CHRISTENSEN

creative director
MARK SEIFERT

STRANGER KISSES TRADE PAPERBACK. November 2001. Published by Avatar Press, Inc.,
9 Triumph Drive Urbana, IL 61802. Stranger Kisses and all related properties TM &
©2001 Warren Ellis. All other characters herein, their distinct likenesses, and related
properties are trademarks of Avatar Press, Inc. The stories, characters, and institutions
mentioned in this magazine are entirely fictional.

stranger kisses™

ONE

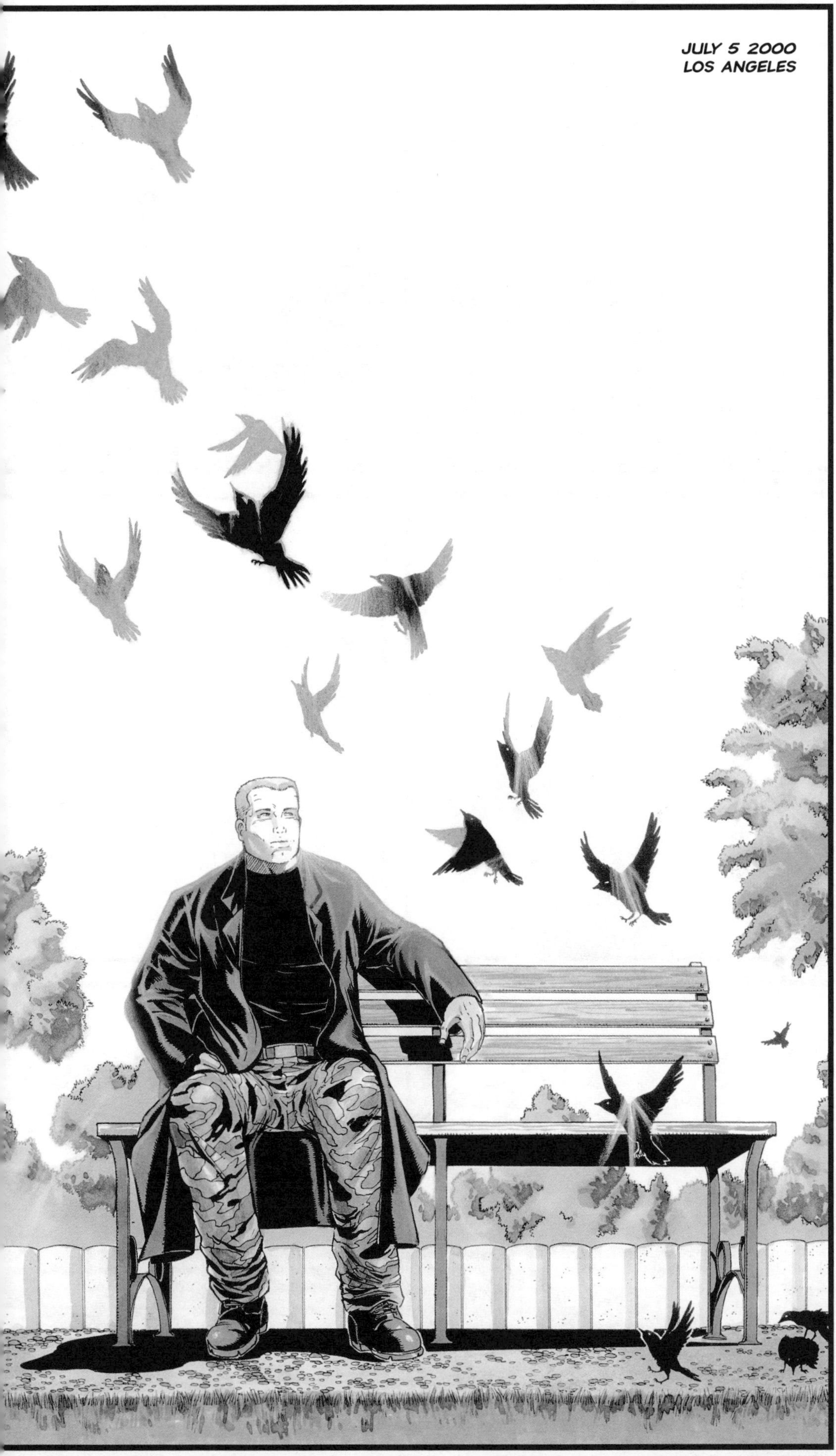
JULY 5 2000
LOS ANGELES

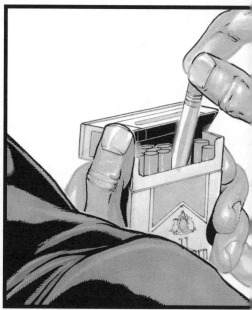

WILLIAM GRAVEL?

HAPPY INDEPENDENCE DAY.

FUCK THE YANKS.

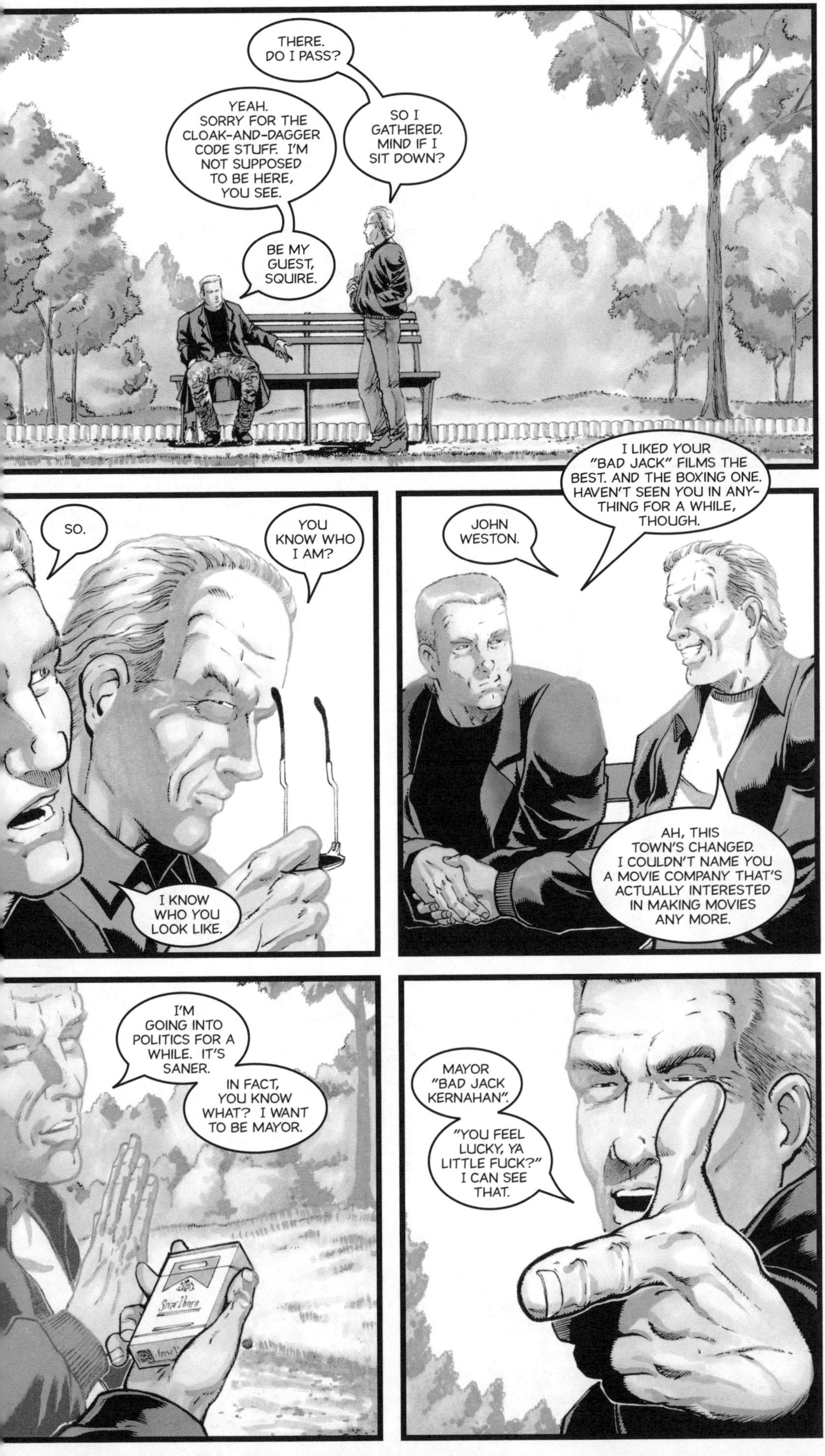
THERE. DO I PASS?
YEAH. SORRY FOR THE CLOAK-AND-DAGGER CODE STUFF. I'M NOT SUPPOSED TO BE HERE, YOU SEE.
SO I GATHERED. MIND IF I SIT DOWN?
BE MY GUEST, SQUIRE.
SO.
YOU KNOW WHO I AM?
I KNOW WHO YOU LOOK LIKE.
JOHN WESTON.
I LIKED YOUR "BAD JACK" FILMS THE BEST. AND THE BOXING ONE. HAVEN'T SEEN YOU IN ANY-THING FOR A WHILE, THOUGH.
AH, THIS TOWN'S CHANGED. I COULDN'T NAME YOU A MOVIE COMPANY THAT'S ACTUALLY INTERESTED IN MAKING MOVIES ANY MORE.
I'M GOING INTO POLITICS FOR A WHILE. IT'S SANER.
IN FACT, YOU KNOW WHAT? I WANT TO BE MAYOR.
MAYOR "BAD JACK KERNAHAN".
"YOU FEEL LUCKY, YA LITTLE FUCK?" I CAN SEE THAT.

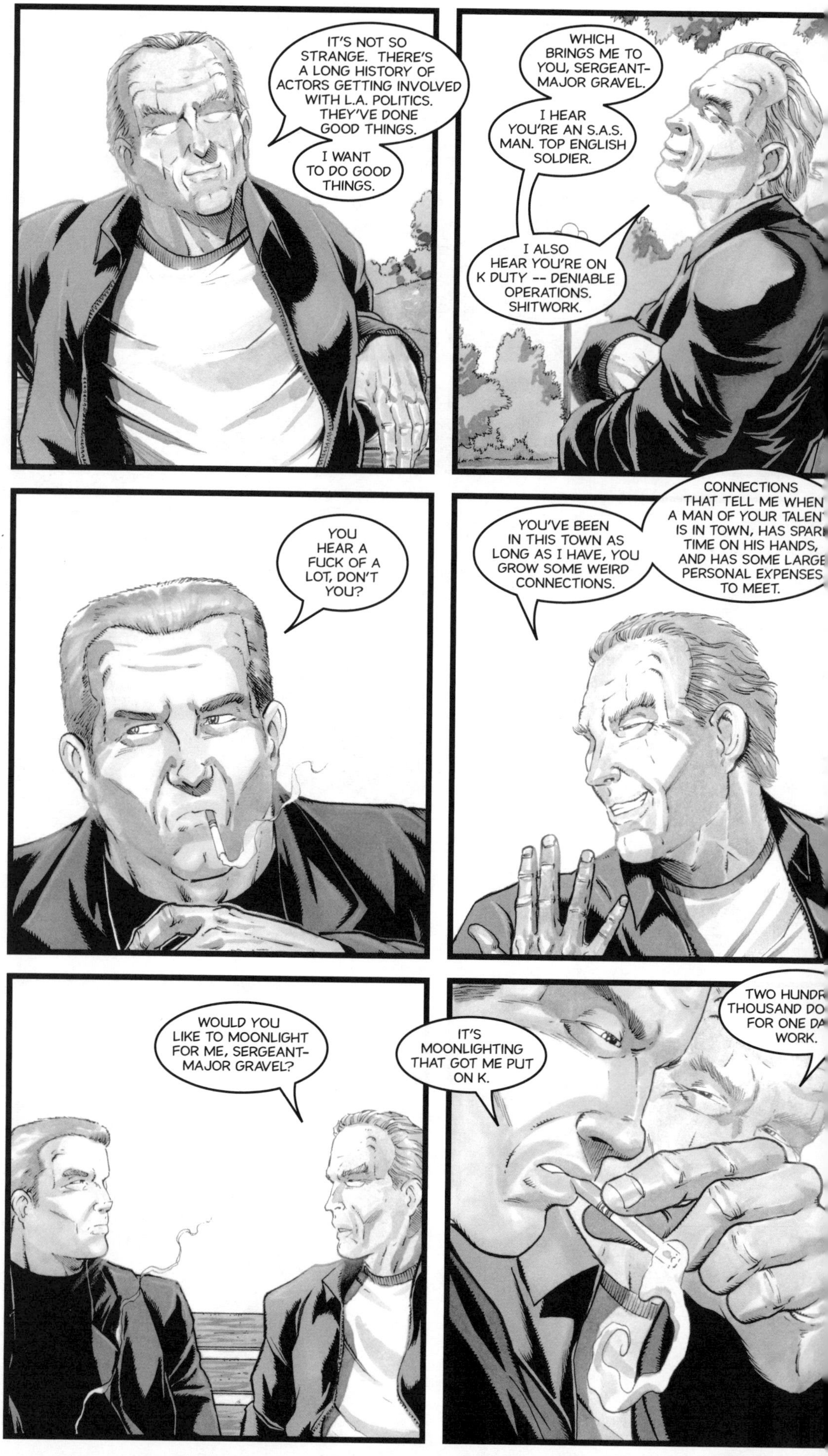
IT'S NOT SO STRANGE. THERE'S A LONG HISTORY OF ACTORS GETTING INVOLVED WITH L.A. POLITICS. THEY'VE DONE GOOD THINGS.
I WANT TO DO GOOD THINGS.
WHICH BRINGS ME TO YOU, SERGEANT-MAJOR GRAVEL.
I HEAR YOU'RE AN S.A.S. MAN. TOP ENGLISH SOLDIER.
I ALSO HEAR YOU'RE ON K DUTY -- DENIABLE OPERATIONS. SHITWORK.
YOU HEAR A FUCK OF A LOT, DON'T YOU?
YOU'VE BEEN IN THIS TOWN AS LONG AS I HAVE, YOU GROW SOME WEIRD CONNECTIONS.
CONNECTIONS THAT TELL ME WHEN A MAN OF YOUR TALEN IS IN TOWN, HAS SPAR TIME ON HIS HANDS, AND HAS SOME LARG PERSONAL EXPENSES TO MEET.
WOULD YOU LIKE TO MOONLIGHT FOR ME, SERGEANT-MAJOR GRAVEL?
IT'S MOONLIGHTING THAT GOT ME PUT ON K.
TWO HUND THOUSAND DO FOR ONE D WORK.

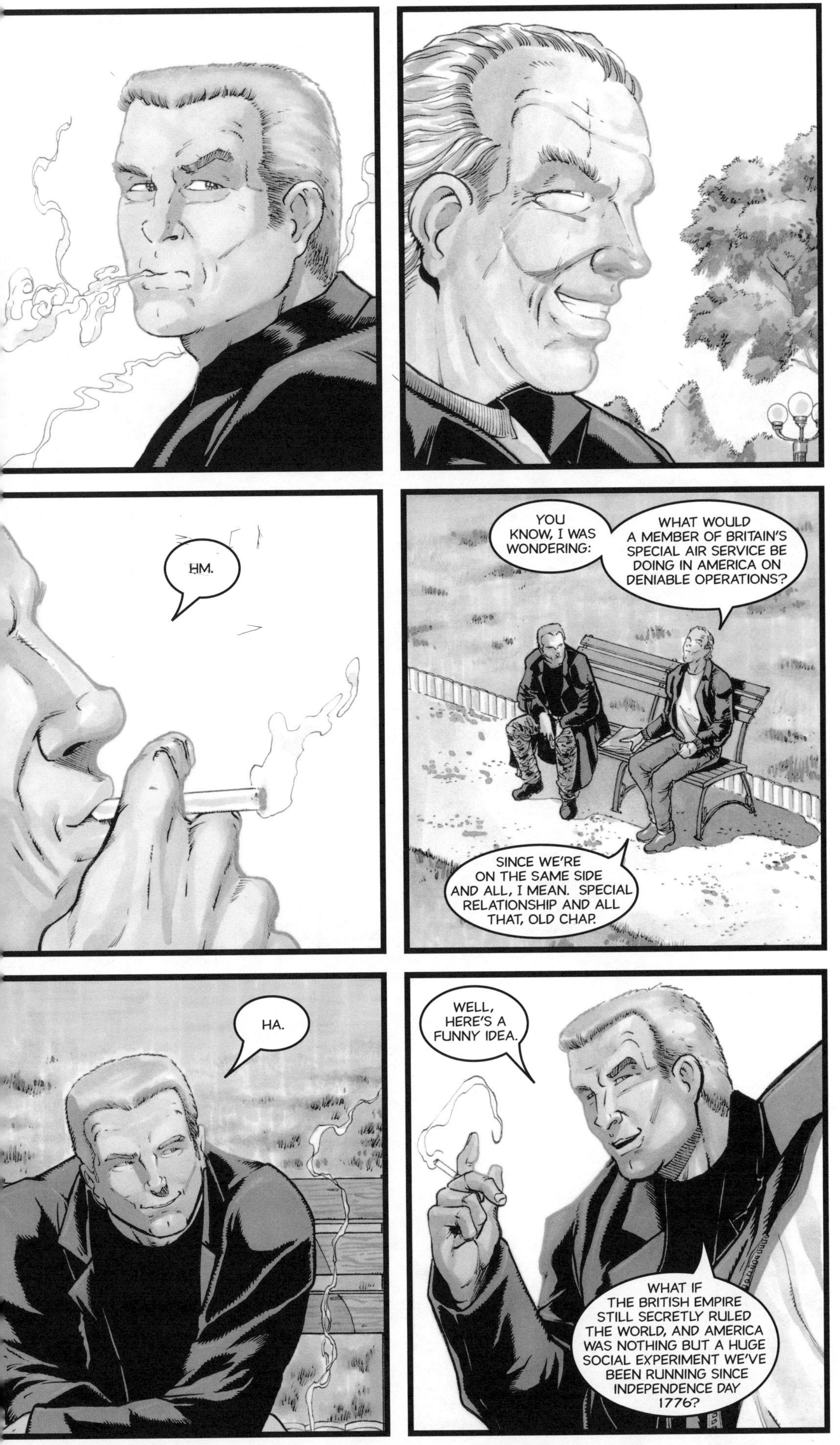
HM.
YOU KNOW, I WAS WONDERING:
WHAT WOULD A MEMBER OF BRITAIN'S SPECIAL AIR SERVICE BE DOING IN AMERICA ON DENIABLE OPERATIONS?
SINCE WE'RE ON THE SAME SIDE AND ALL, I MEAN. SPECIAL RELATIONSHIP AND ALL THAT, OLD CHAP.
HA.
WELL, HERE'S A FUNNY IDEA.
WHAT IF THE BRITISH EMPIRE STILL SECRETLY RULED THE WORLD, AND AMERICA WAS NOTHING BUT A HUGE SOCIAL EXPERIMENT WE'VE BEEN RUNNING SINCE INDEPENDENCE DAY 1776?

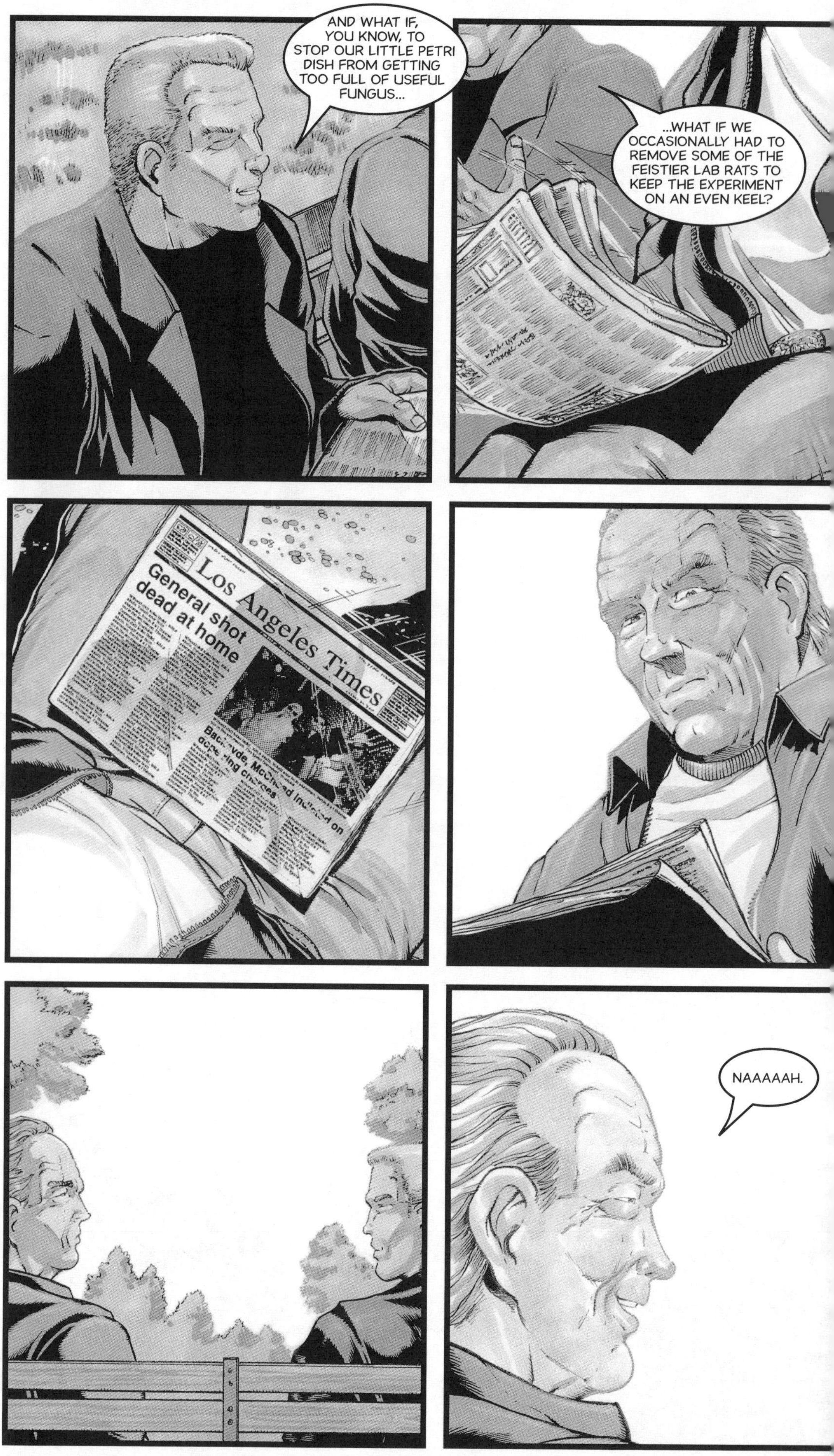
AND WHAT IF, YOU KNOW, TO STOP OUR LITTLE PETRI DISH FROM GETTING TOO FULL OF USEFUL FUNGUS...
...WHAT IF WE OCCASIONALLY HAD TO REMOVE SOME OF THE FEISTIER LAB RATS TO KEEP THE EXPERIMENT ON AN EVEN KEEL?
Los Angeles Times
General shot dead at home
NAAAAAH.

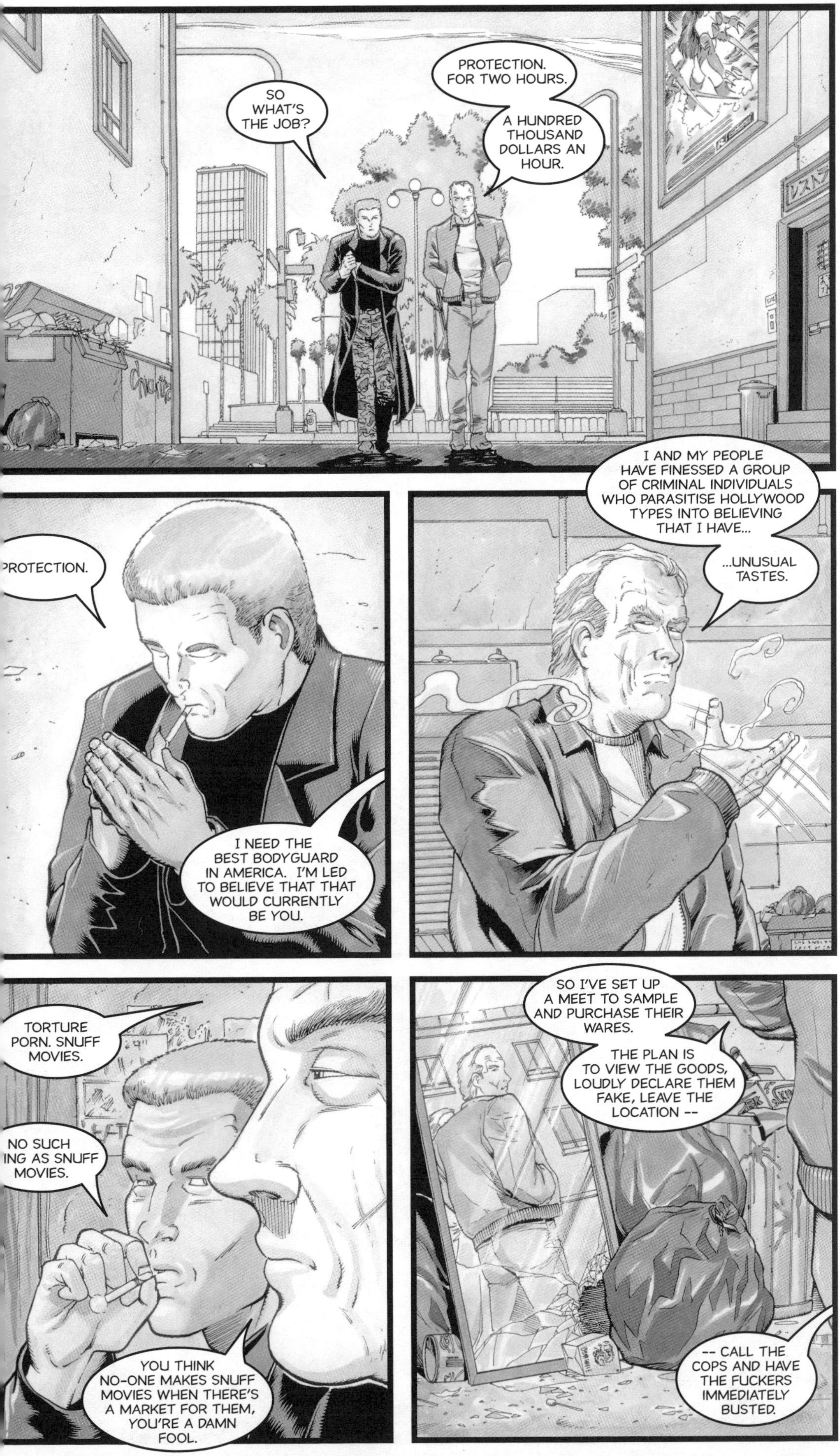
SO WHAT'S THE JOB?
PROTECTION. FOR TWO HOURS.
A HUNDRED THOUSAND DOLLARS AN HOUR.
PROTECTION.
I NEED THE BEST BODYGUARD IN AMERICA. I'M LED TO BELIEVE THAT THAT WOULD CURRENTLY BE YOU.
I AND MY PEOPLE HAVE FINESSED A GROUP OF CRIMINAL INDIVIDUALS WHO PARASITISE HOLLYWOOD TYPES INTO BELIEVING THAT I HAVE...
...UNUSUAL TASTES.
TORTURE PORN. SNUFF MOVIES.
NO SUCH
ING AS SNUFF MOVIES.
YOU THINK NO-ONE MAKES SNUFF MOVIES WHEN THERE'S A MARKET FOR THEM, YOU'RE A DAMN FOOL.
SO I'VE SET UP A MEET TO SAMPLE AND PURCHASE THEIR WARES.
THE PLAN IS TO VIEW THE GOODS, LOUDLY DECLARE THEM FAKE, LEAVE THE LOCATION --
-- CALL THE COPS AND HAVE THE FUCKERS IMMEDIATELY BUSTED.

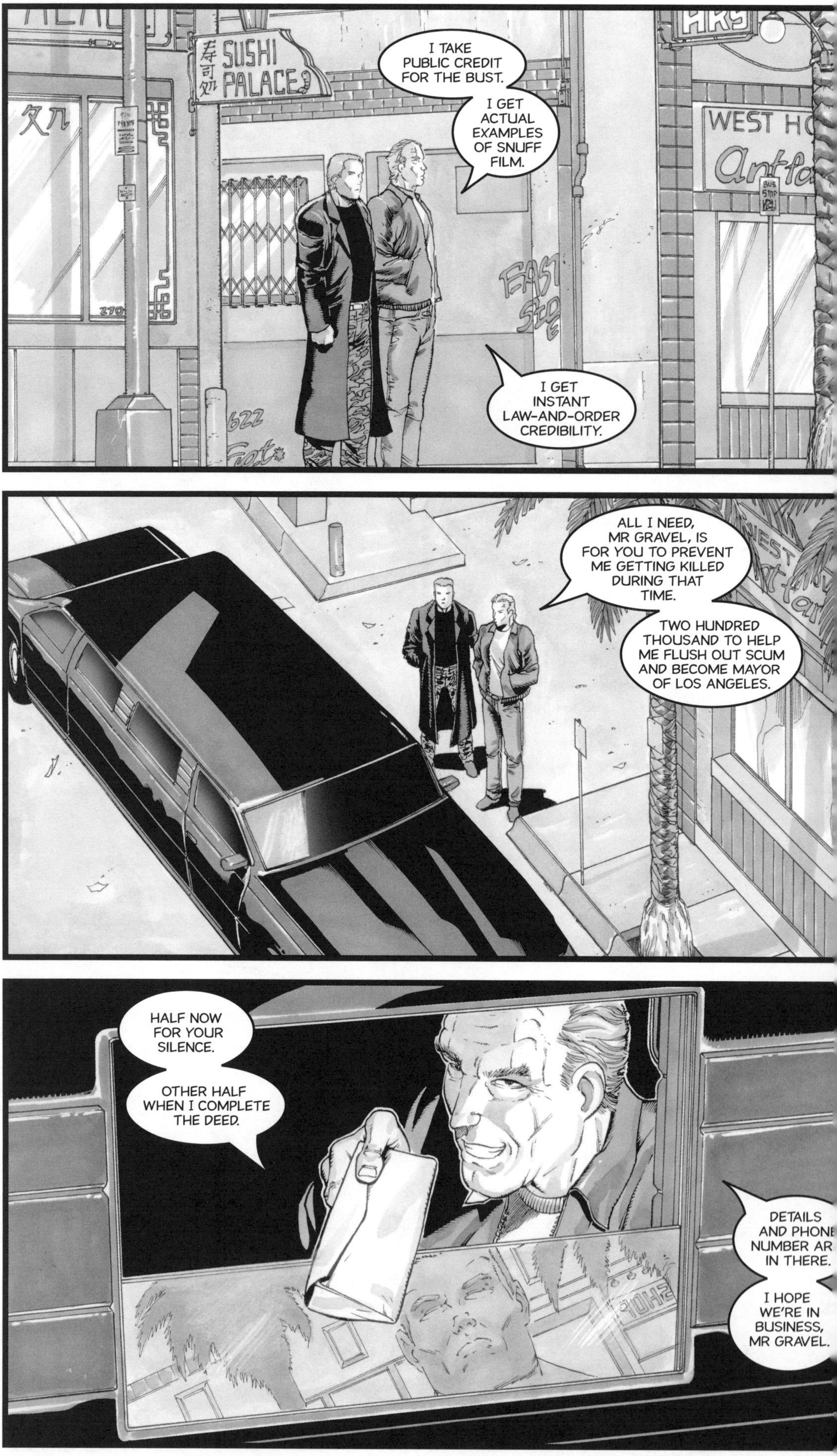

SUSHI PALACE
I TAKE PUBLIC CREDIT FOR THE BUST.
I GET ACTUAL EXAMPLES OF SNUFF FILM.
I GET INSTANT LAW-AND-ORDER CREDIBILITY.
ALL I NEED, MR GRAVEL, IS FOR YOU TO PREVENT ME GETTING KILLED DURING THAT TIME.
TWO HUNDRED THOUSAND TO HELP ME FLUSH OUT SCUM AND BECOME MAYOR OF LOS ANGELES.
HALF NOW FOR YOUR SILENCE.
OTHER HALF WHEN I COMPLETE THE DEED.
DETAILS AND PHONE NUMBER AR IN THERE.
I HOPE WE'RE IN BUSINESS, MR GRAVEL.

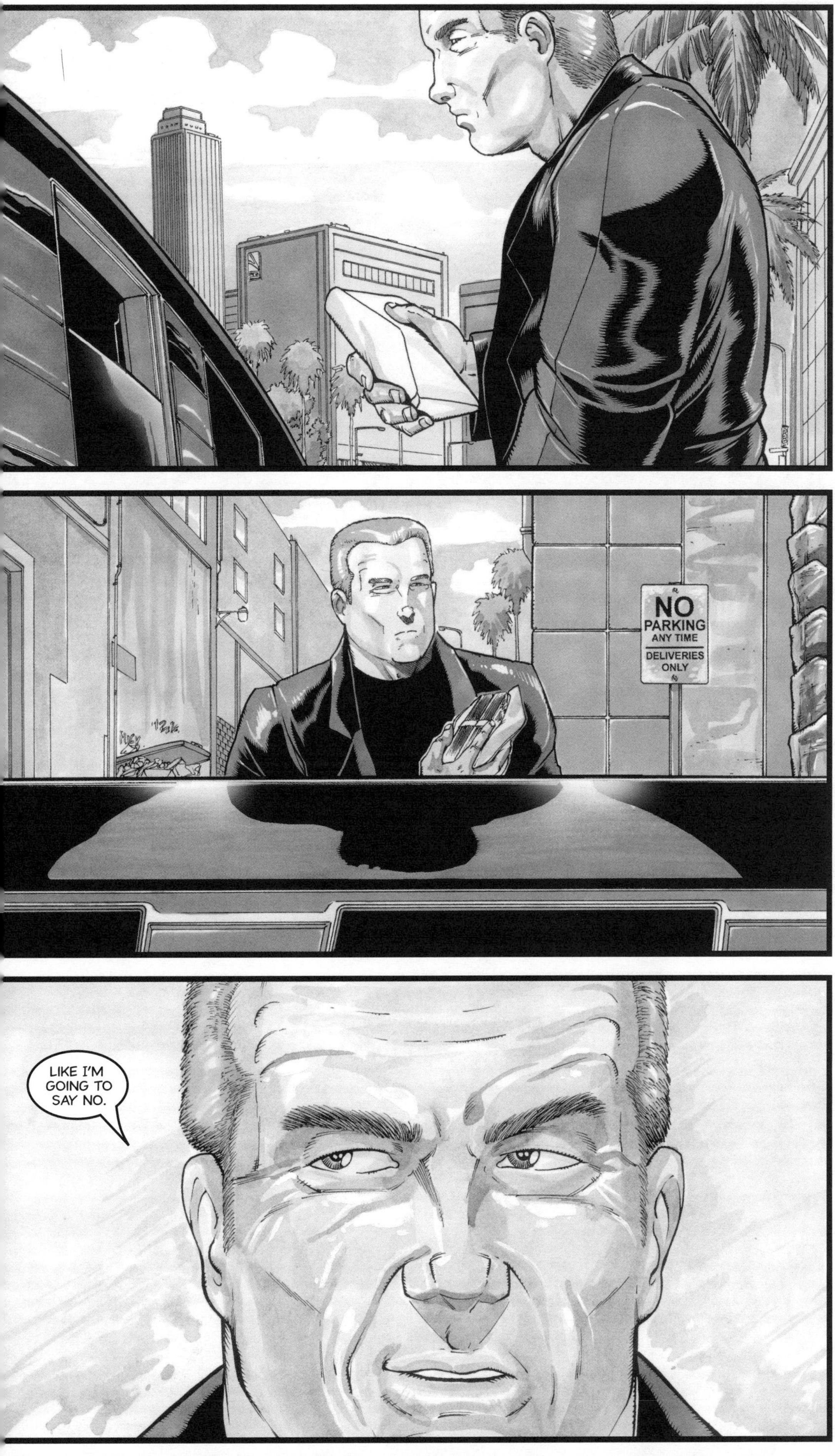
NO PARKING
ANY TIME
DELIVERIES ONLY
LIKE I'M GOING TO SAY NO.

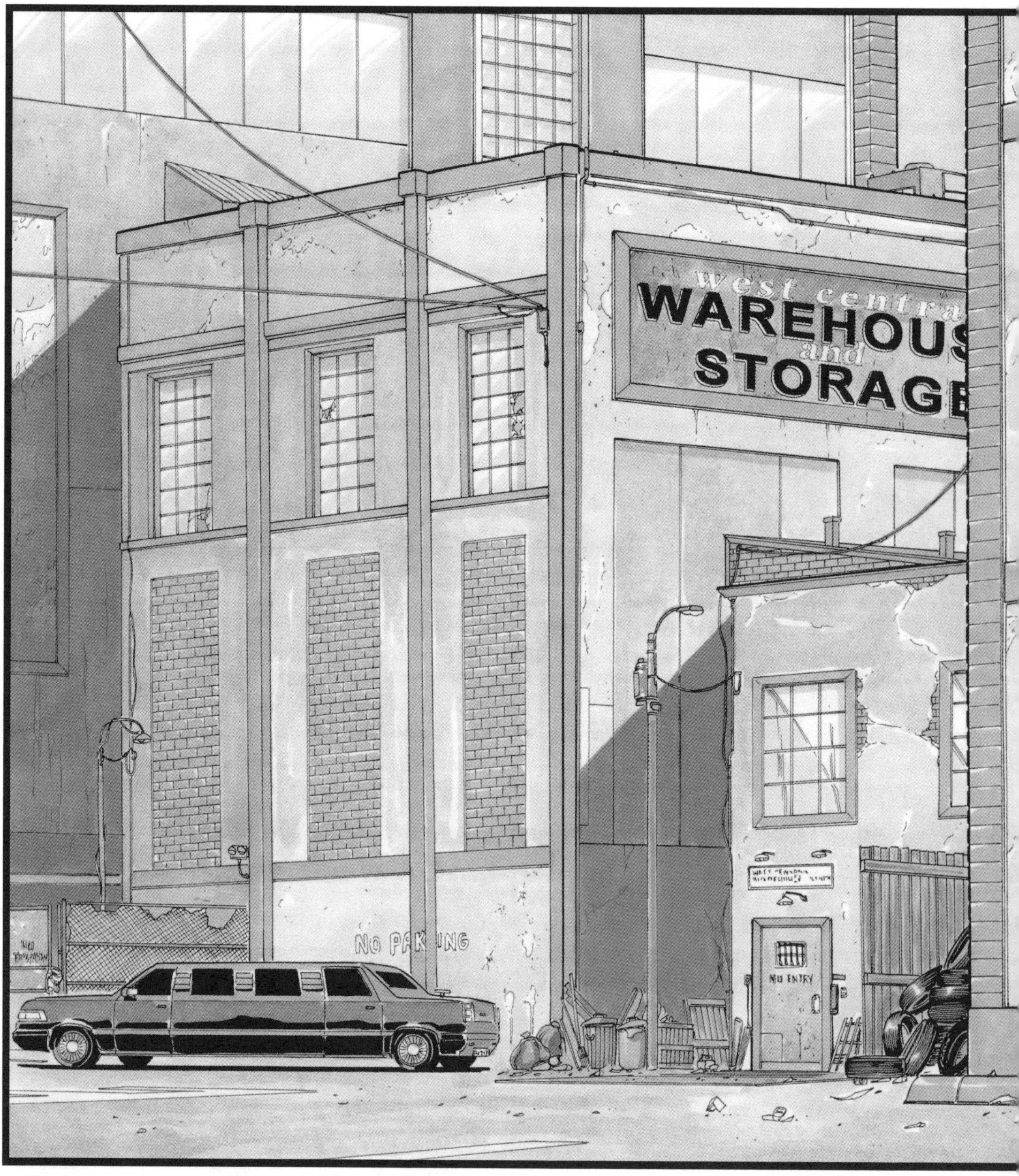
west centra
WAREHOUS
and
STORAGE
NO ENTRY

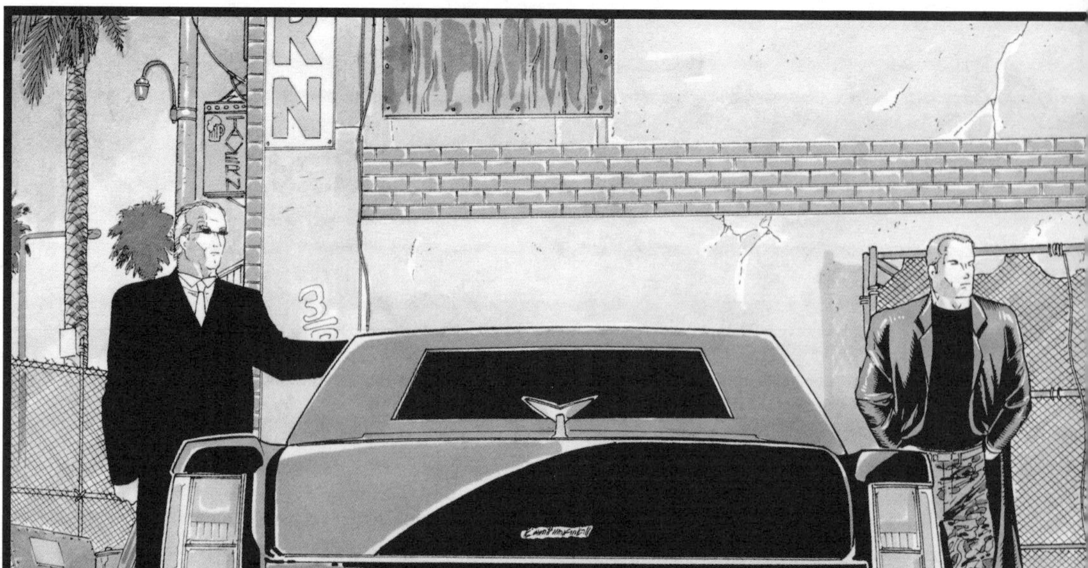
RN
TAVERN

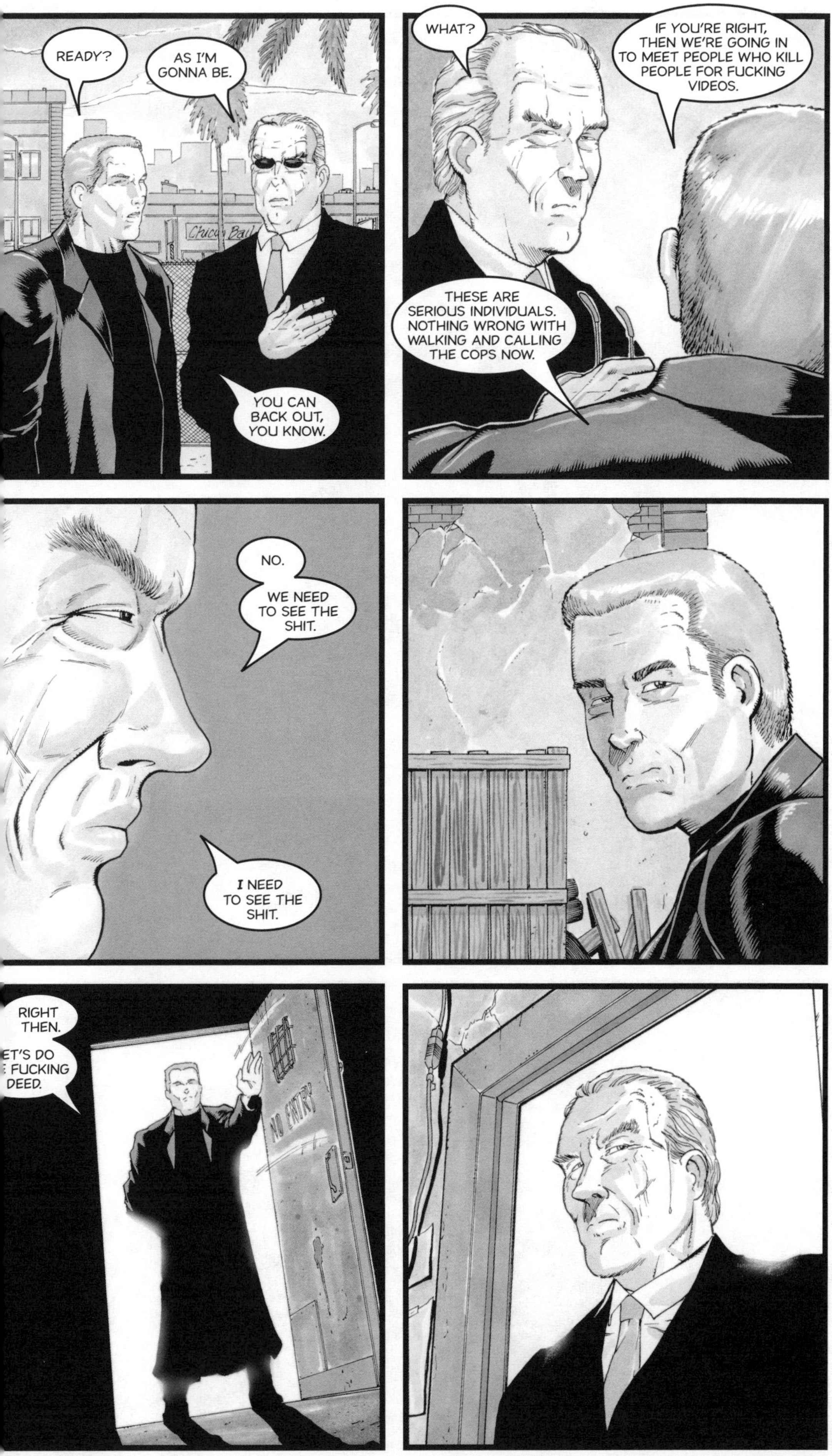
READY?
AS I'M GONNA BE.
YOU CAN BACK OUT, YOU KNOW.
WHAT?
IF YOU'RE RIGHT, THEN WE'RE GOING IN TO MEET PEOPLE WHO KILL PEOPLE FOR FUCKING VIDEOS.
THESE ARE SERIOUS INDIVIDUALS. NOTHING WRONG WITH WALKING AND CALLING THE COPS NOW.
NO.
WE NEED TO SEE THE SHIT.
I NEED TO SEE THE SHIT.
RIGHT THEN.
ET'S DO FUCKING DEED.
NO ENTRY

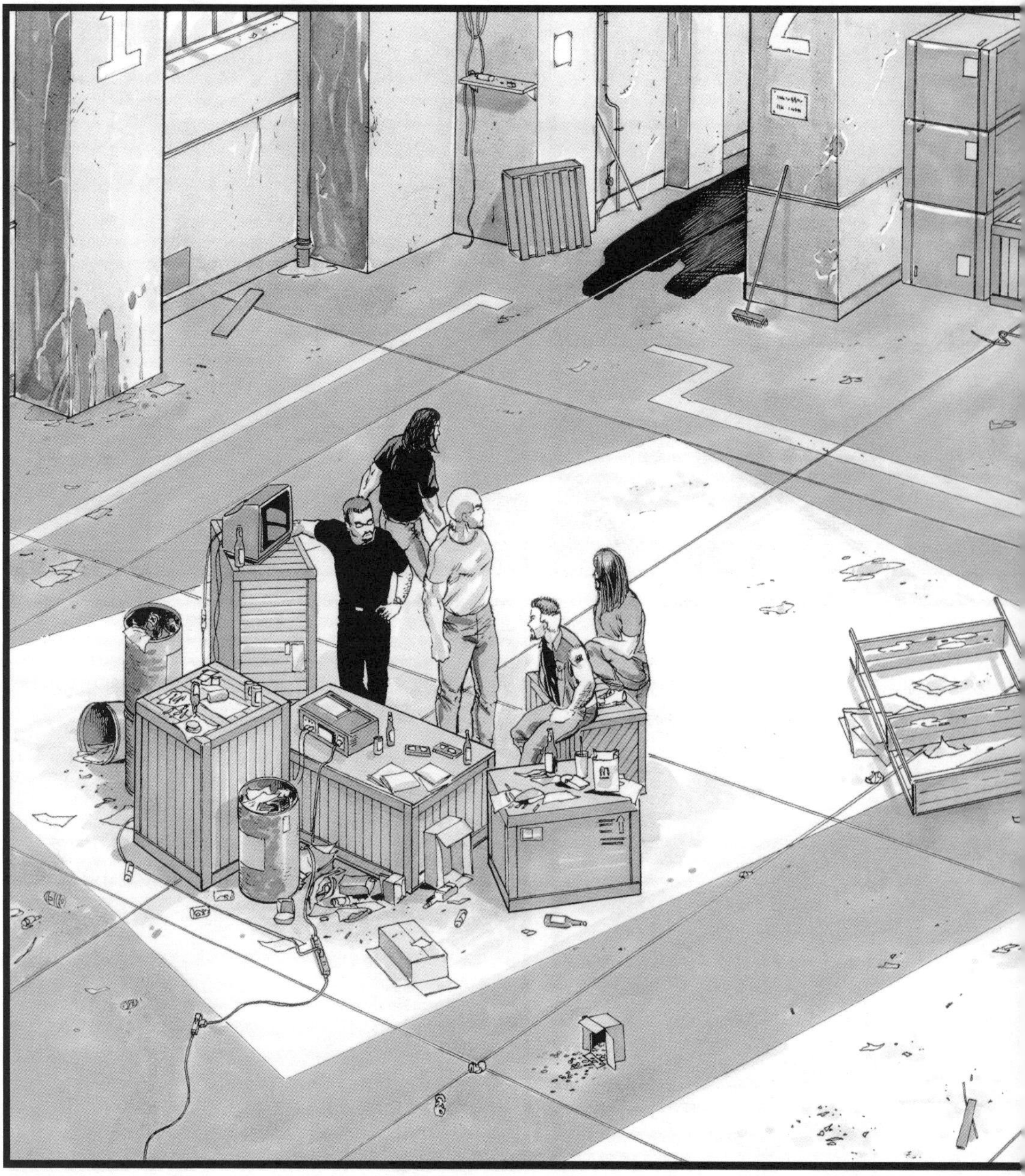

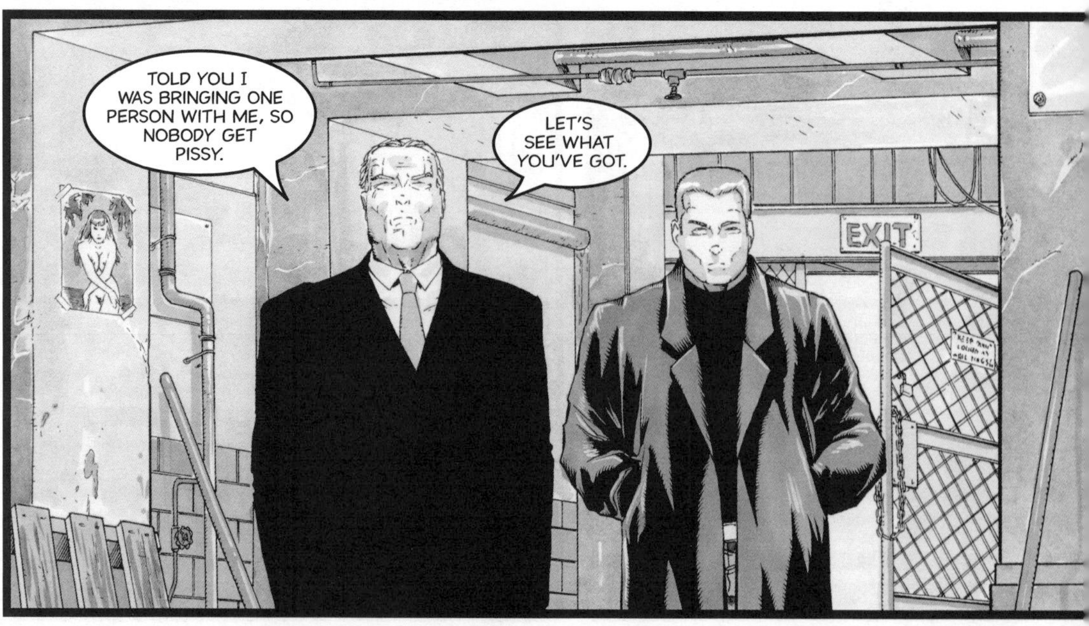
TOLD YOU I WAS BRINGING ONE PERSON WITH ME, SO NOBODY GET PISSY.
LET'S SEE WHAT YOU'VE GOT.
EXIT

YOU CARRYIN'?

FUCK OFF.

LEMME SEE WHAT YOU'RE CARRYIN'.

FUCK OFF.

CUNT.

SHOW ME THE FUCKIN' GUN RIGHT NOW.

I'M HERE PROTECTION. XPLAIN IT TO CKFACE HERE R I'M GOING O KILL HIM.

LITTLE FUCK, MY DAUGHTER IS BIGGER AND SCARIER THAN YOU.

AND SHE HAS NO LEGS AND A CRACK HABIT.

DO AS YOU'RE TOLD.

GIVE ME THE FUCKIN' GUN, ASSWIPE --

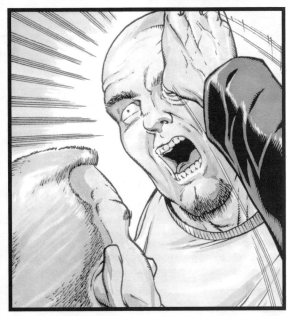

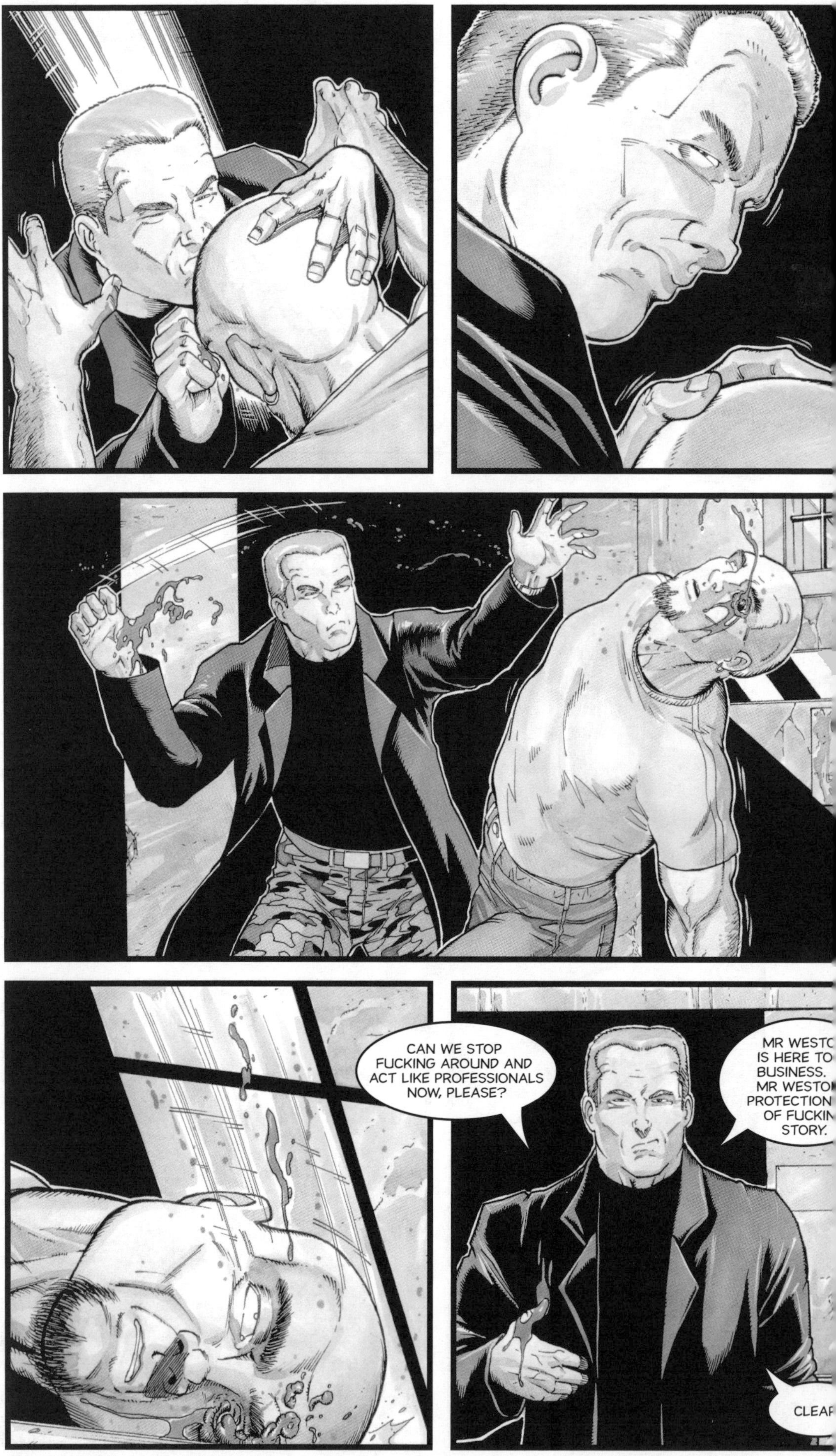
CAN WE STOP FUCKING AROUND AND ACT LIKE PROFESSIONALS NOW, PLEASE?
MR WESTO IS HERE TO BUSINESS. MR WESTO PROTECTION OF FUCKIN STORY.
CLEAR

AND I
NT TO SEE
HE GOODS
BEFORE
I BUY.

YOUR BEHAVIOR
TOWARDS MY FRIEND
HERE HAS MADE ME
DISTRUST YOU. MAKE
ME HAPPY AGAIN.

OKAY.

BUT YOU
UNDERSTAND,
ONCE YOU SEE WHAT WE
HAVE AND WHAT SERVICES
WE PROVIDE, YOU ARE
UNDER *OBLIGATIONS.*

JUST PLAY
THE TAPE.

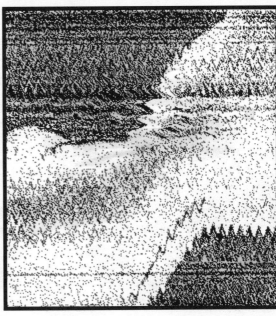

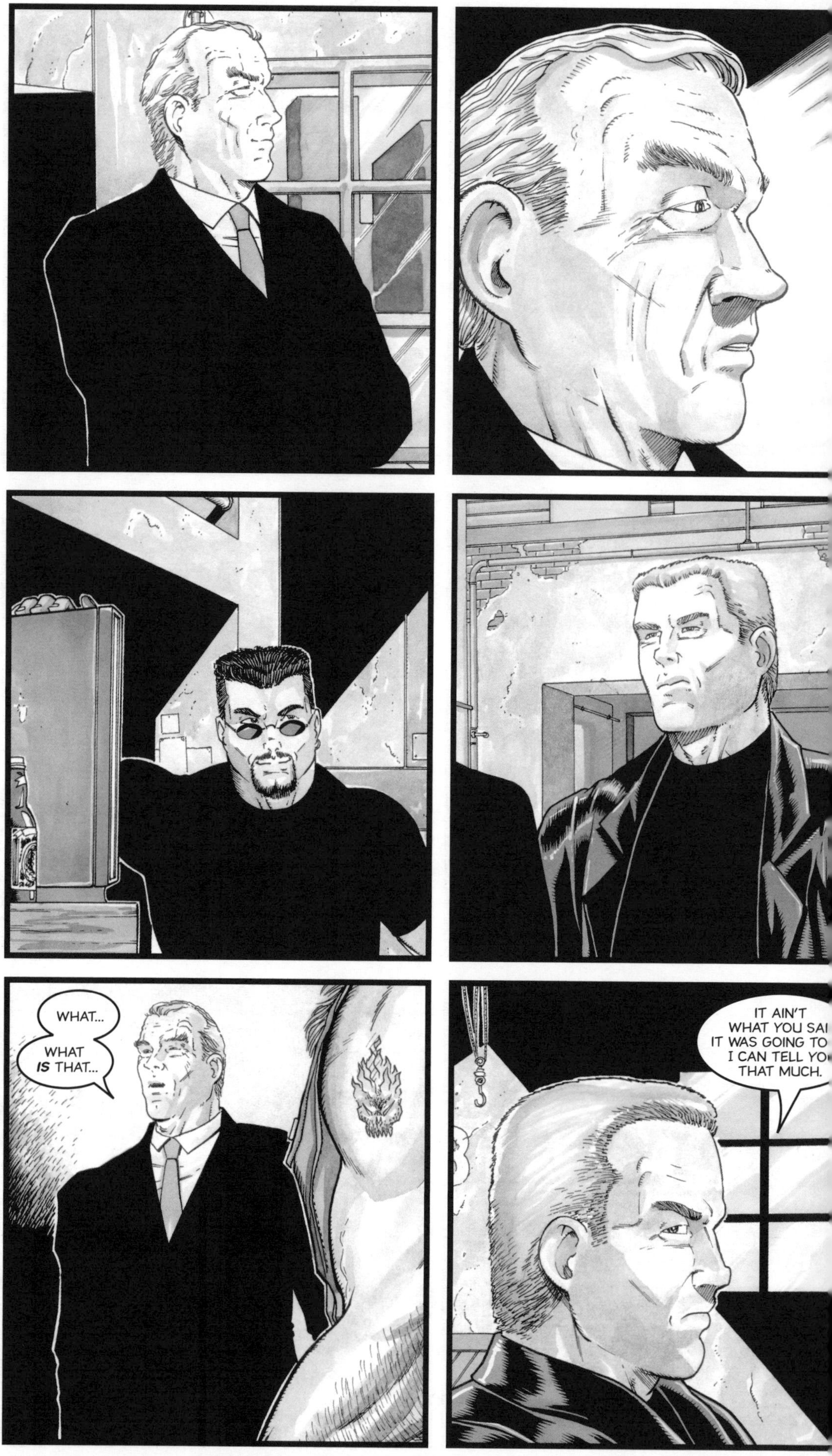
WHAT...
WHAT IS THAT...
IT AIN'T
WHAT YOU SAI
IT WAS GOING TO
I CAN TELL YO
THAT MUCH.

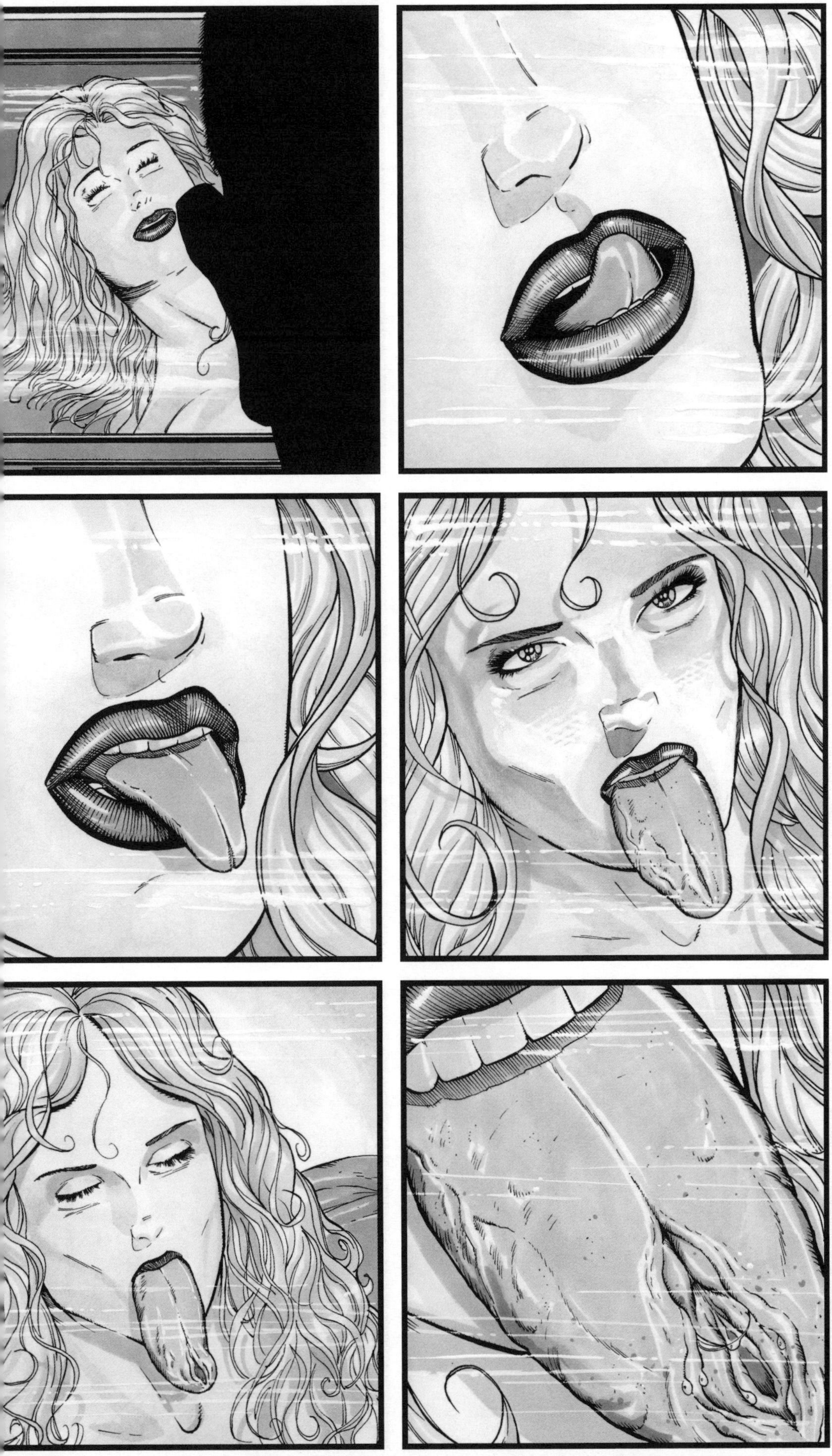

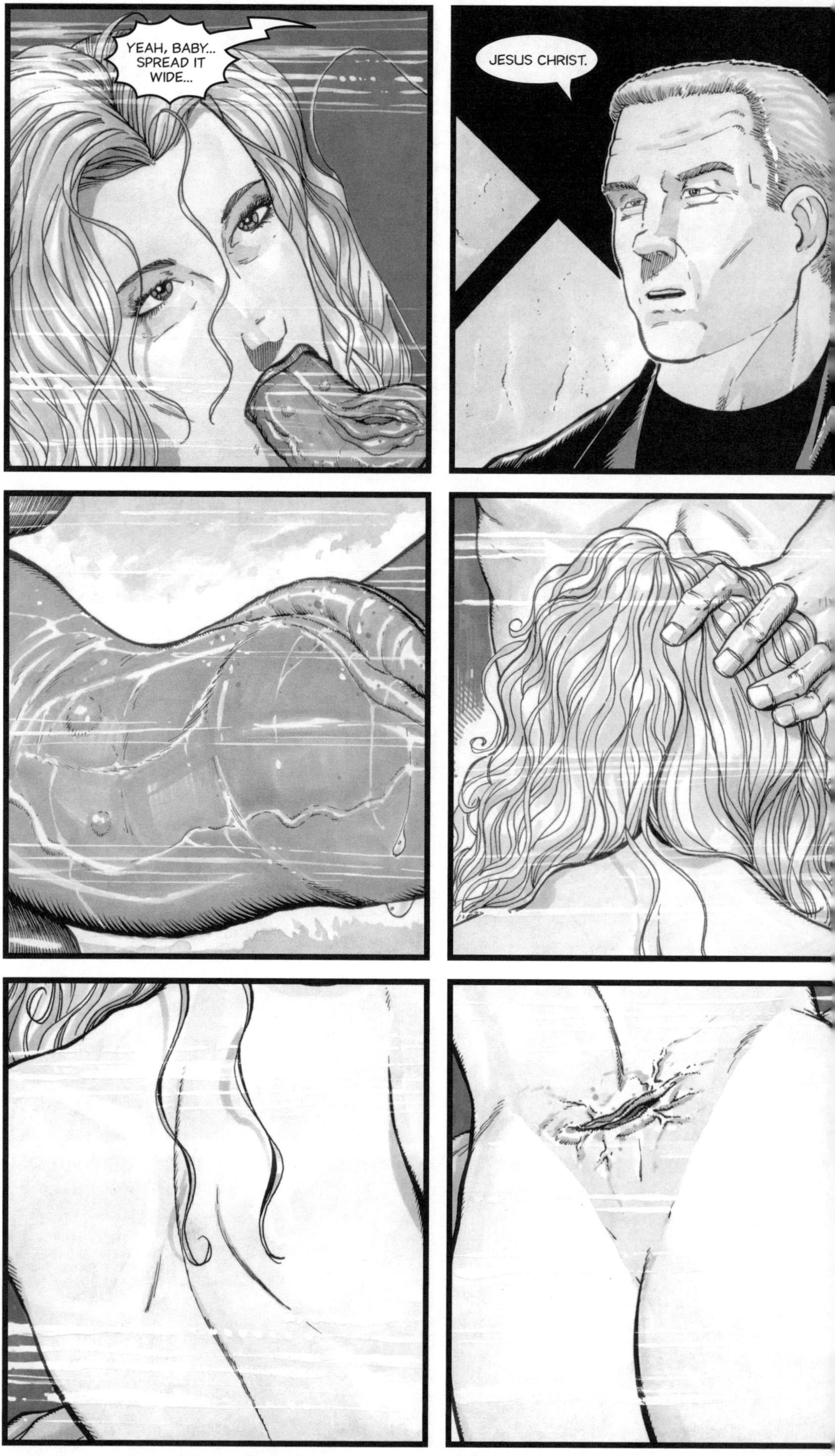
YEAH, BABY... SPREAD IT WIDE...
JESUS CHRIST.

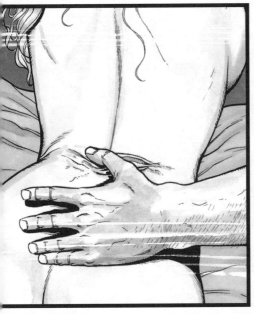

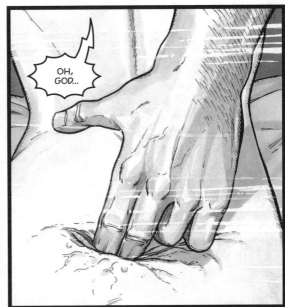

OH, GOD...

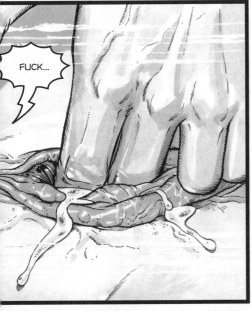

FUCK...

THIS ISN'T...

THIS ISN'T WHAT WE TALKED ABOUT...

UNUSUAL TASTES, YOU SAID. WE DELIVER.

THIS IS WHAT THE REAL MOVERS AND SHAKERS IN HOLLYWOOD LIKE. THIS IS WHAT WE CATER TO.

SOMETHING THAT GETS YOU RICH STRANGE FOLK OFF. SOMETHING THAT IS EXPENSIVE, AND COSTS PEOPLE AND MONEY.

THOUGHT WE WERE TALKING ABOUT THE SAME THING. THAT YOU KNEW THE 411 HERE.

I GUESS YOU'RE NOT BOX OFFICE GOLD ANYMORE, HUH?

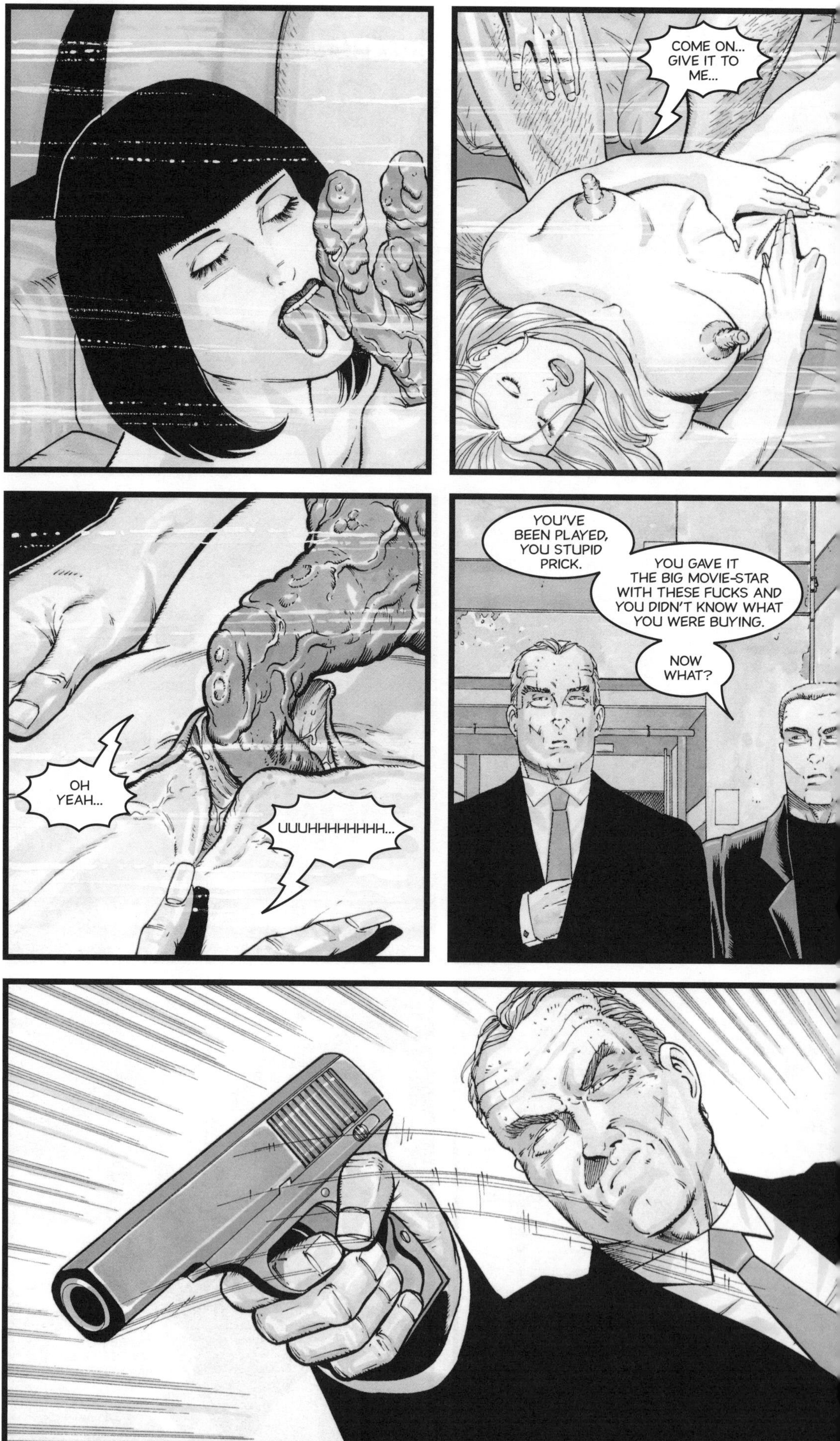
COME ON... GIVE IT TO ME...
OH YEAH...
UUUHHHHHHHH...
YOU'VE BEEN PLAYED, YOU STUPID PRICK.
YOU GAVE IT THE BIG MOVIE-STAR WITH THESE FUCKS AND YOU DIDN'T KNOW WHAT YOU WERE BUYING.
NOW WHAT?

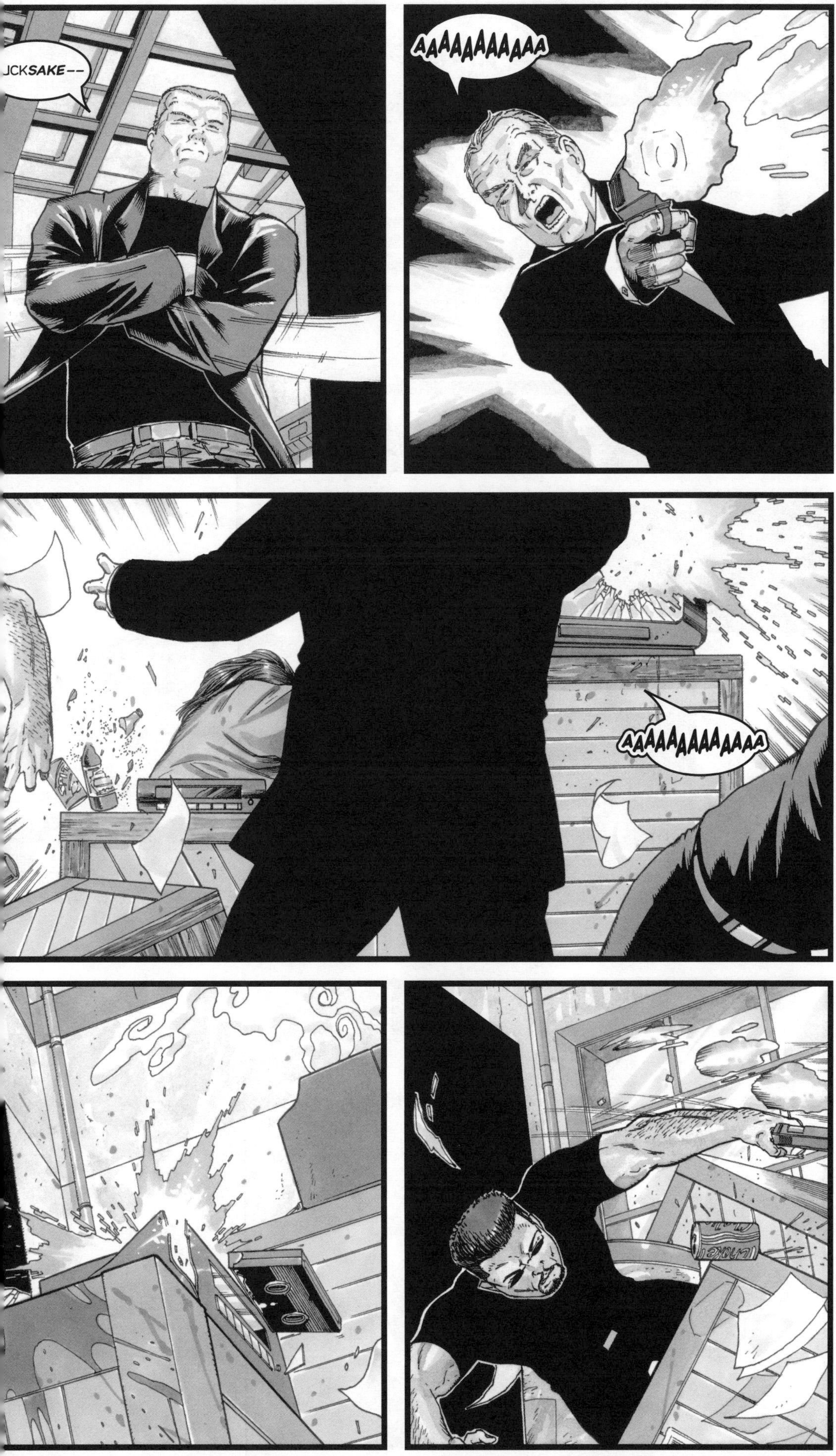
JCKSAKE--
AAAAAAAAAAA
AAAAAAAAAAAA

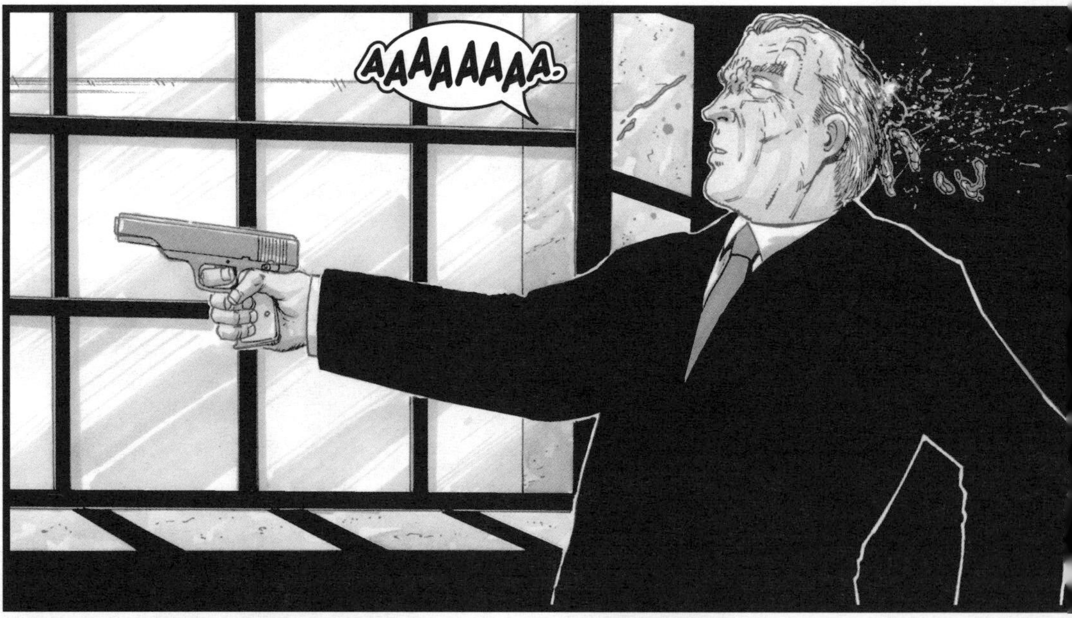
AAAAAAAA.
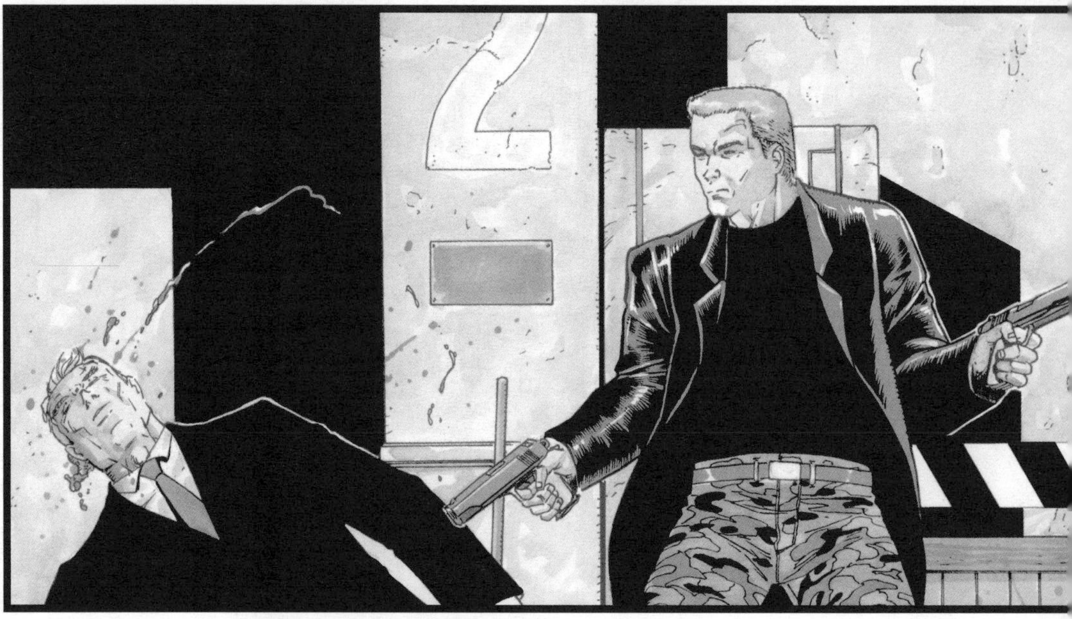
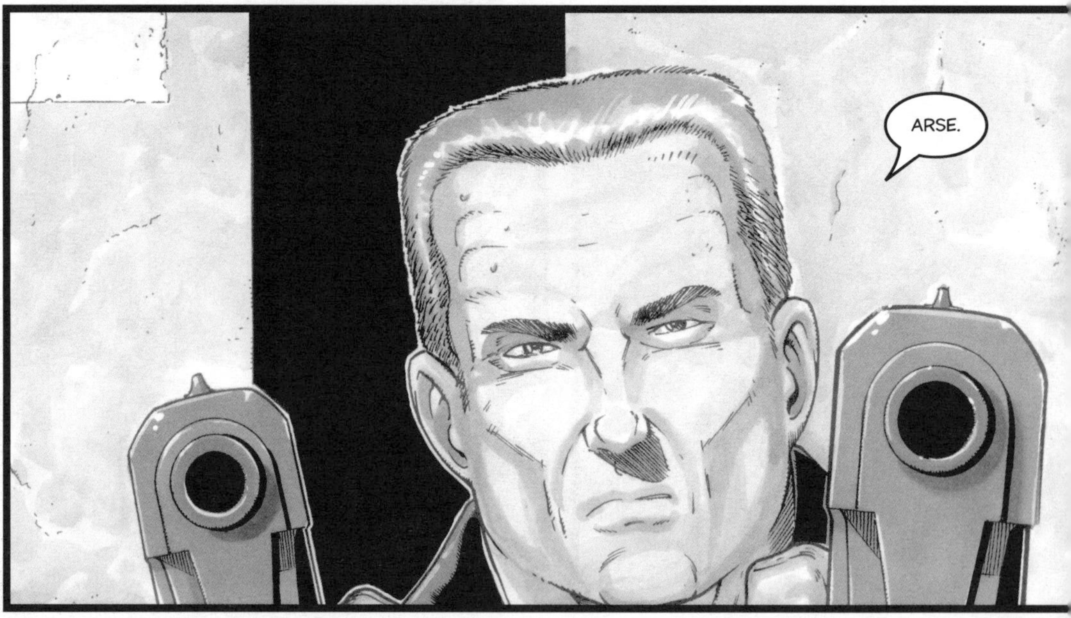
ARSE.

stranger kisses™

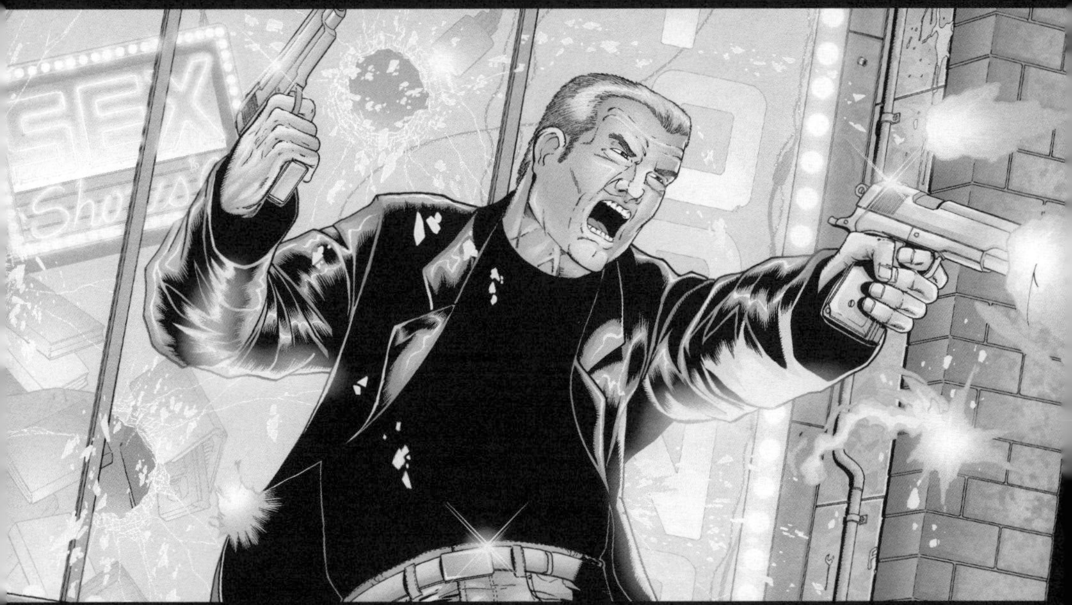
SEX

TWO

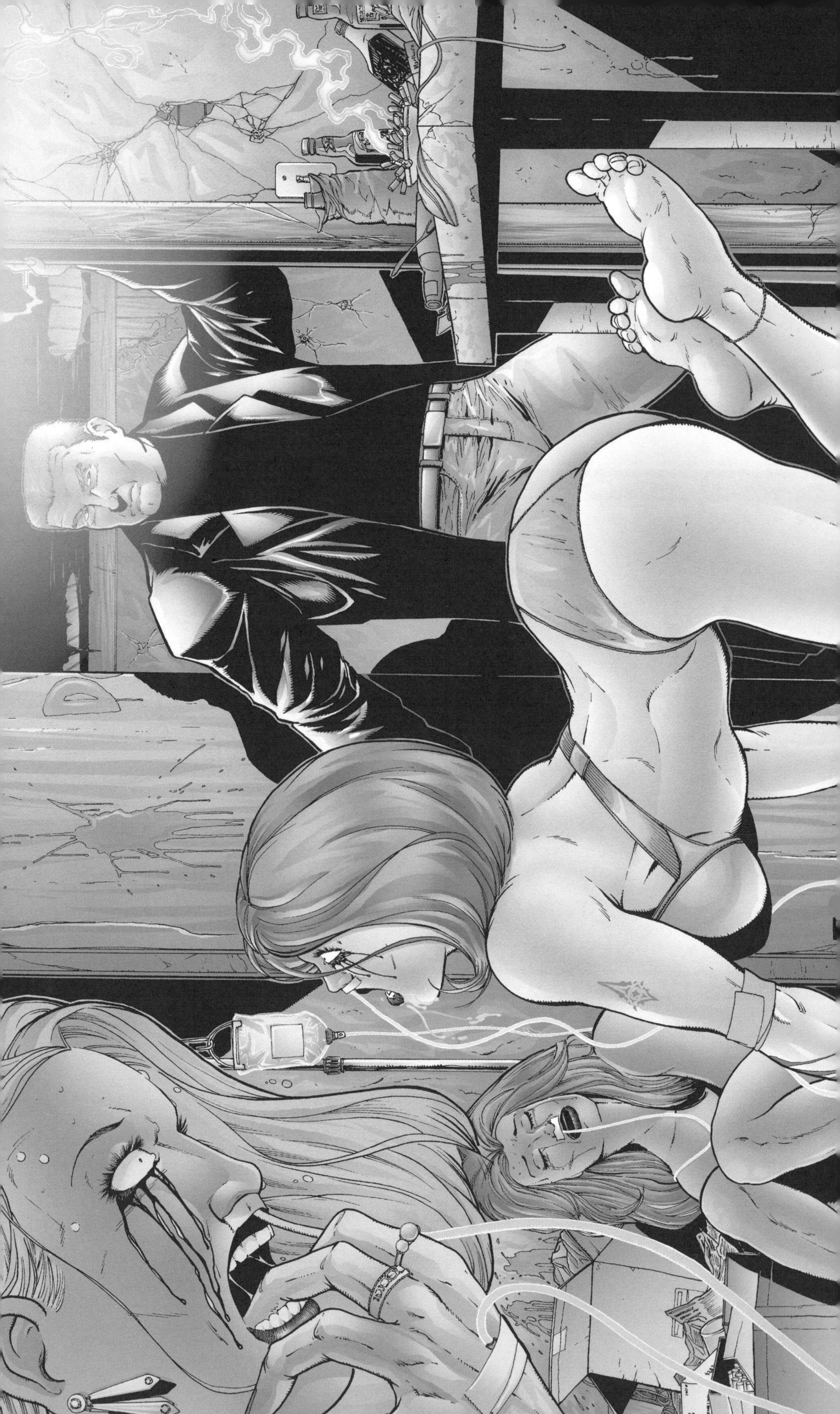

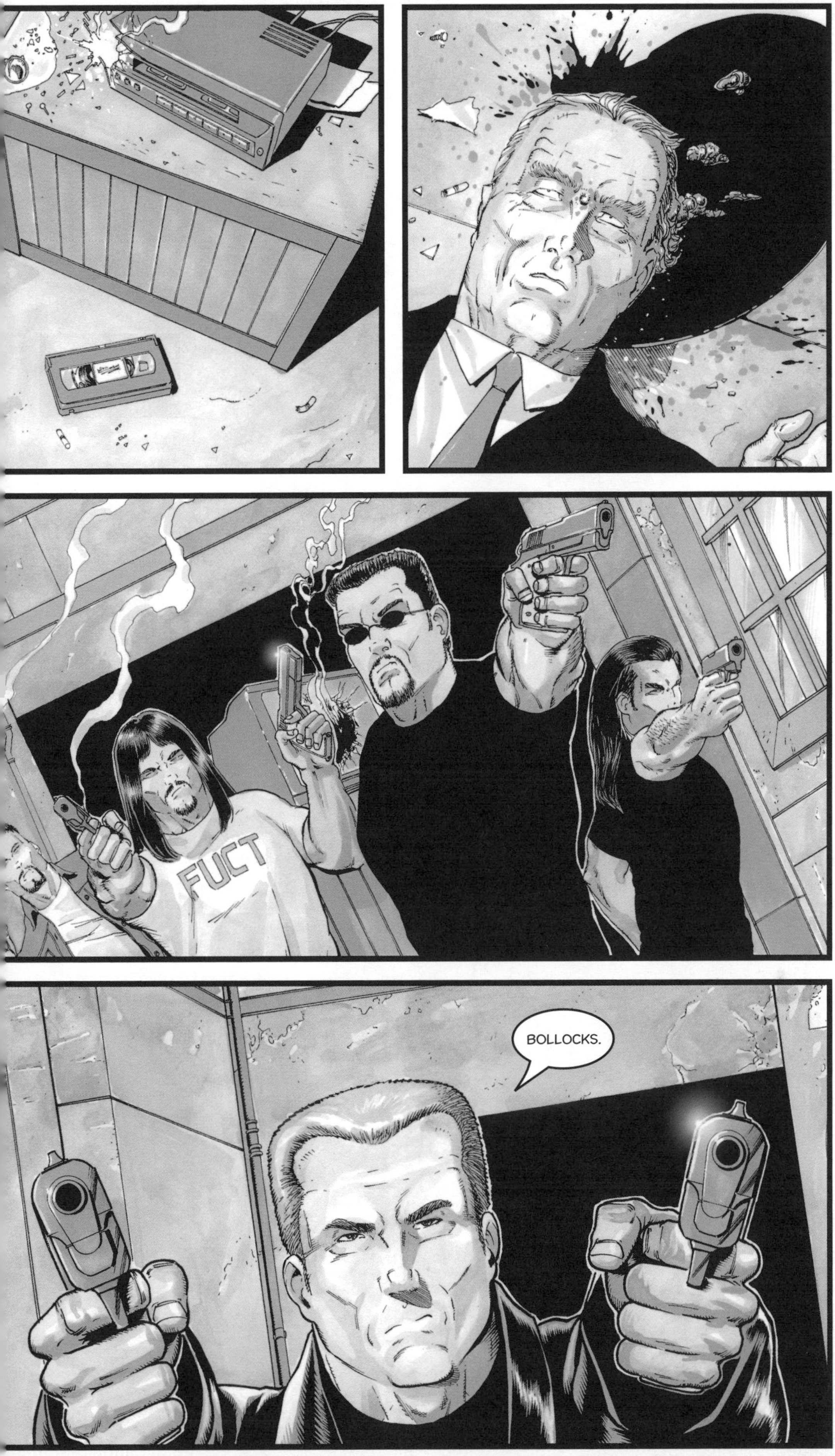
FUCT
BOLLOCKS.

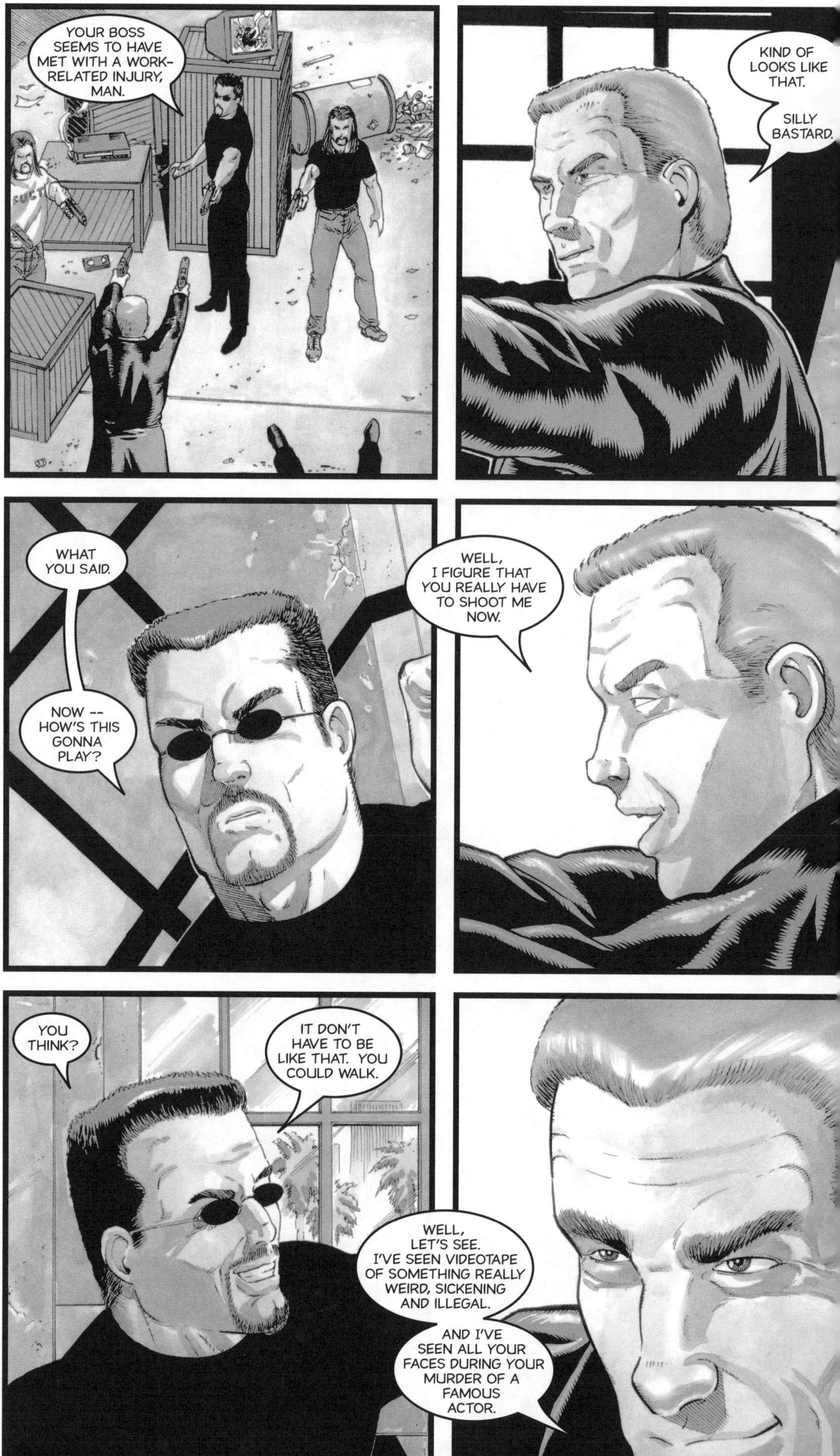
YOUR BOSS SEEMS TO HAVE MET WITH A WORK-RELATED INJURY, MAN.
KIND OF LOOKS LIKE THAT.
SILLY BASTARD.
WHAT YOU SAID.
NOW -- HOW'S THIS GONNA PLAY?
WELL, I FIGURE THAT YOU REALLY HAVE TO SHOOT ME NOW.
YOU THINK?
IT DON'T HAVE TO BE LIKE THAT. YOU COULD WALK.
WELL, LET'S SEE. I'VE SEEN VIDEOTAPE OF SOMETHING REALLY WEIRD, SICKENING AND ILLEGAL.
AND I'VE SEEN ALL YOUR FACES DURING YOUR MURDER OF A FAMOUS ACTOR.

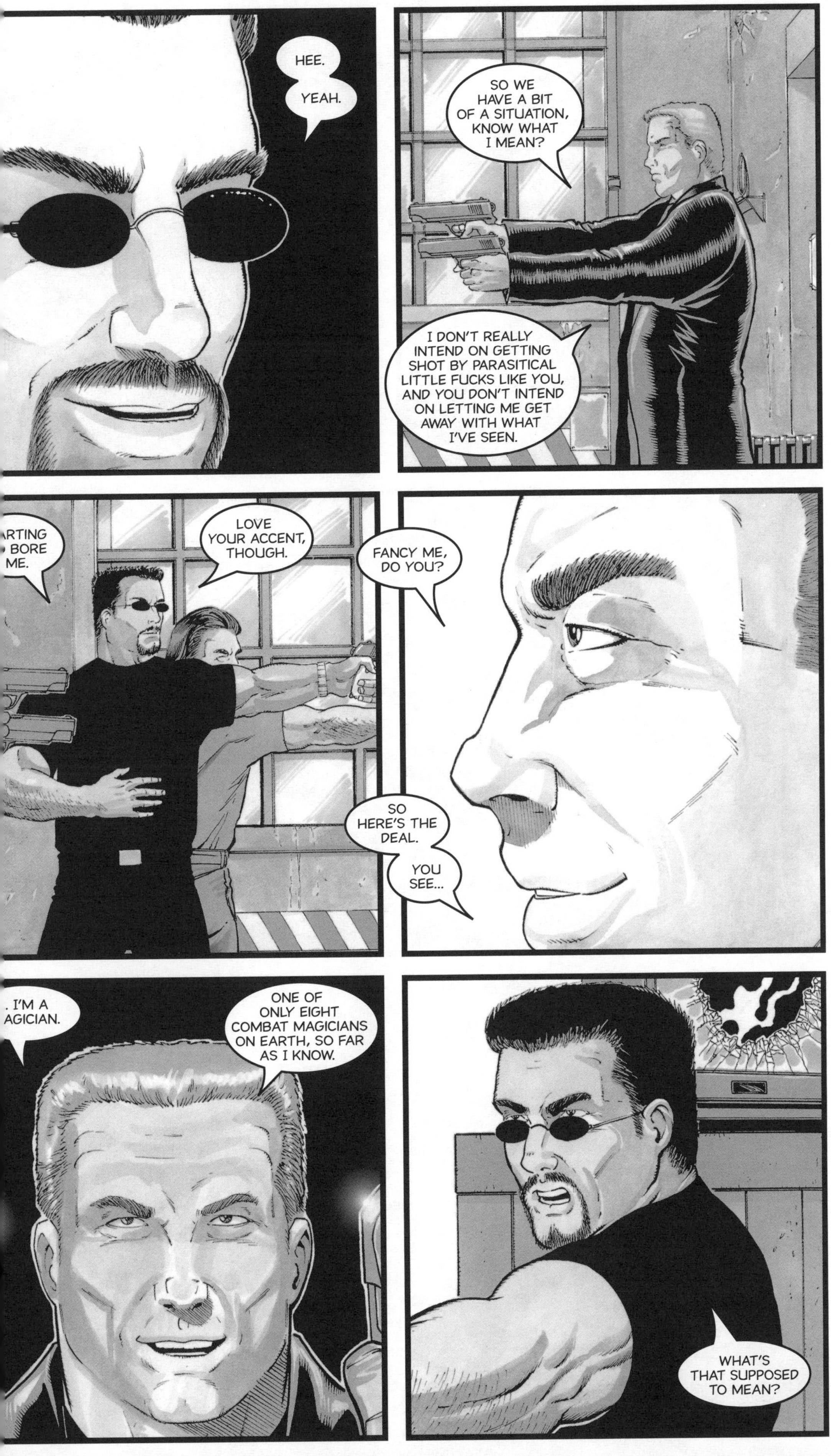
HEE.
YEAH.
SO WE HAVE A BIT OF A SITUATION, KNOW WHAT I MEAN?
I DON'T REALLY INTEND ON GETTING SHOT BY PARASITICAL LITTLE FUCKS LIKE YOU, AND YOU DON'T INTEND ON LETTING ME GET AWAY WITH WHAT I'VE SEEN.
ARTING BORE ME.
LOVE YOUR ACCENT, THOUGH.
FANCY ME, DO YOU?
SO HERE'S THE DEAL.
YOU SEE...
I'M A AGICIAN.
ONE OF ONLY EIGHT COMBAT MAGICIANS ON EARTH, SO FAR AS I KNOW.
WHAT'S THAT SUPPOSED TO MEAN?

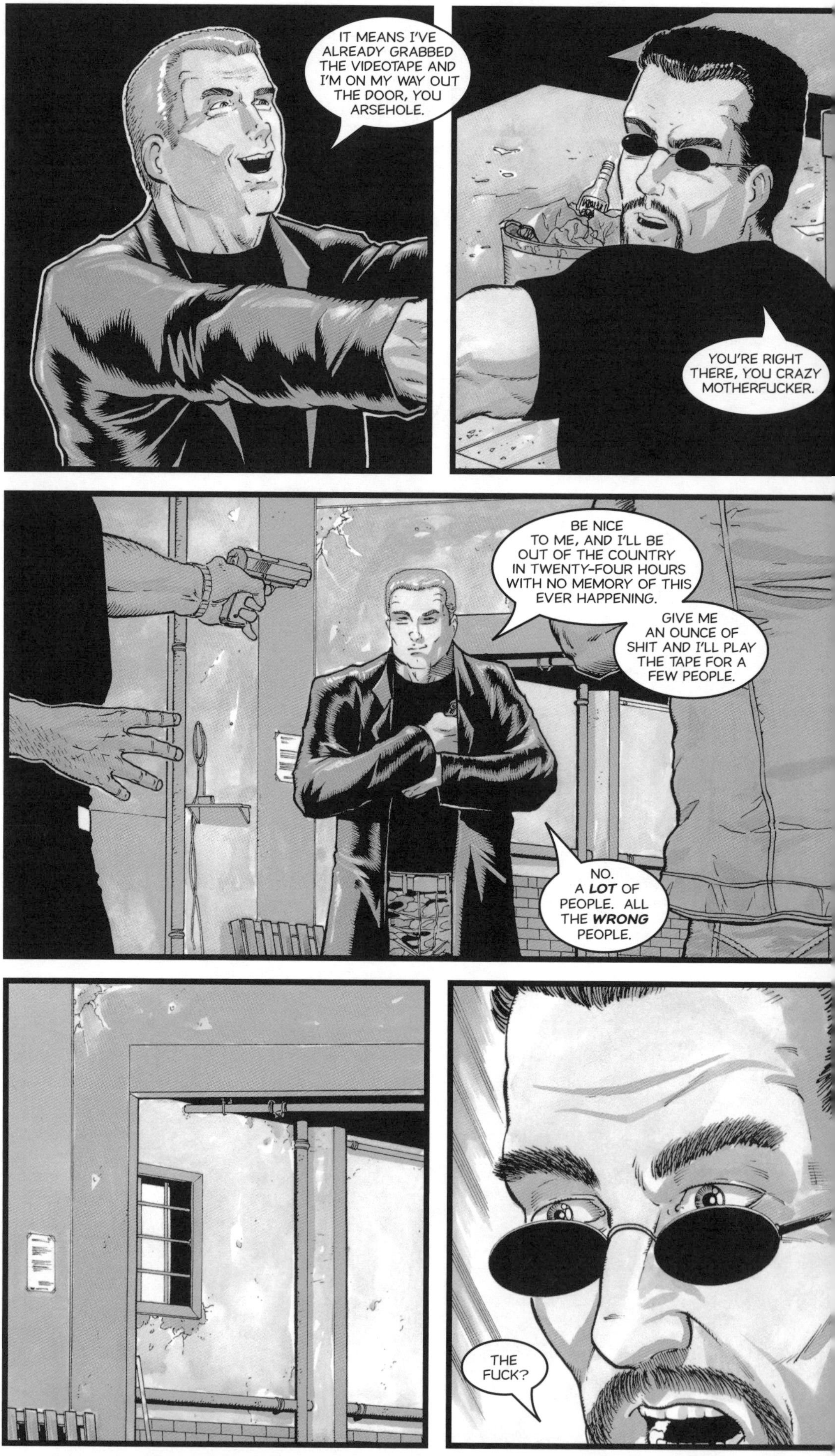
IT MEANS I'VE ALREADY GRABBED THE VIDEOTAPE AND I'M ON MY WAY OUT THE DOOR, YOU ARSEHOLE.
YOU'RE RIGHT THERE, YOU CRAZY MOTHERFUCKER.
BE NICE TO ME, AND I'LL BE OUT OF THE COUNTRY IN TWENTY-FOUR HOURS WITH NO MEMORY OF THIS EVER HAPPENING.
GIVE ME AN OUNCE OF SHIT AND I'LL PLAY THE TAPE FOR A FEW PEOPLE.
NO. A LOT OF PEOPLE. ALL THE WRONG PEOPLE.
THE FUCK?

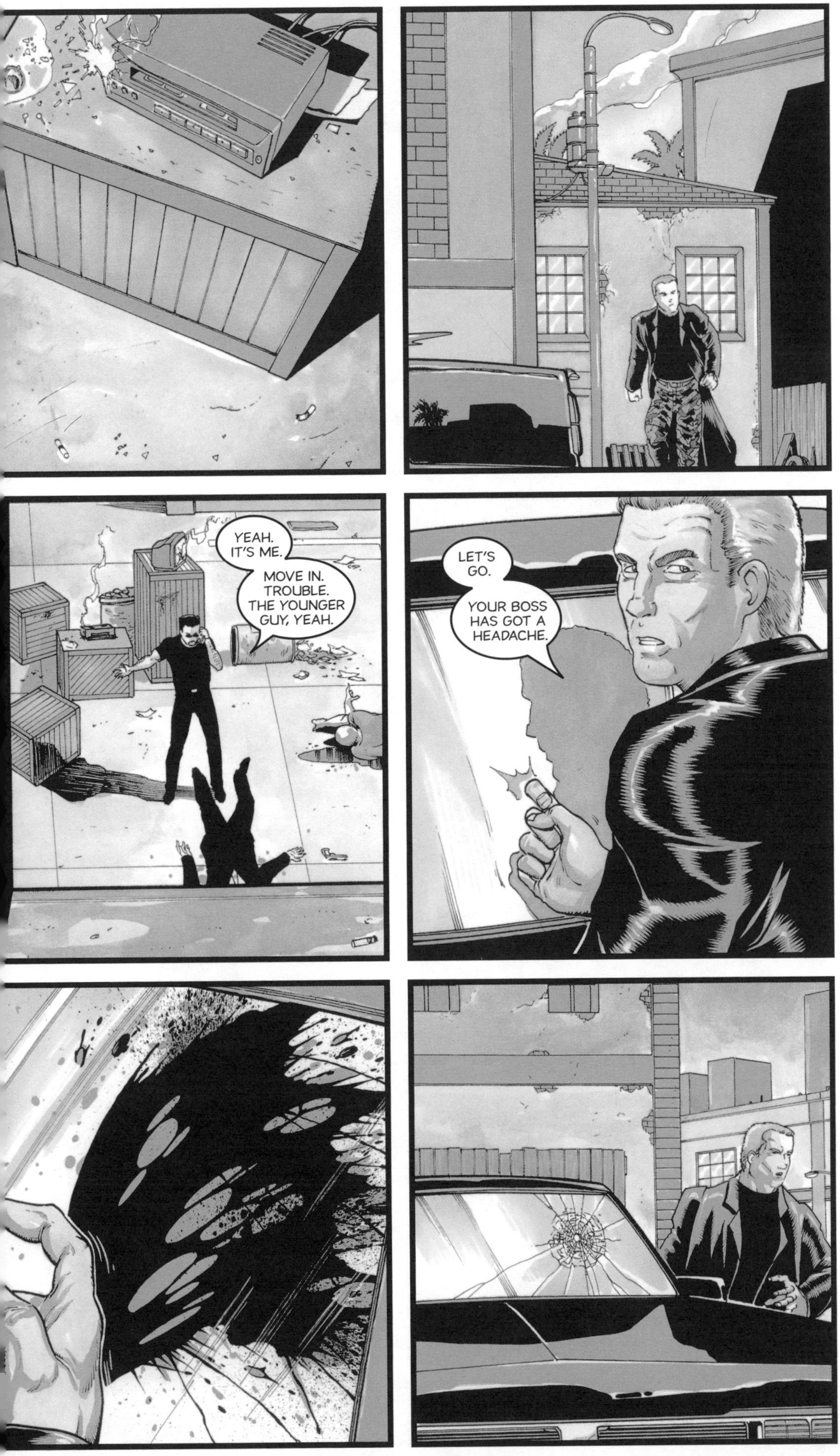
YEAH. IT'S ME.
MOVE IN. TROUBLE. THE YOUNGER GUY, YEAH.
LET'S GO.
YOUR BOSS HAS GOT A HEADACHE.

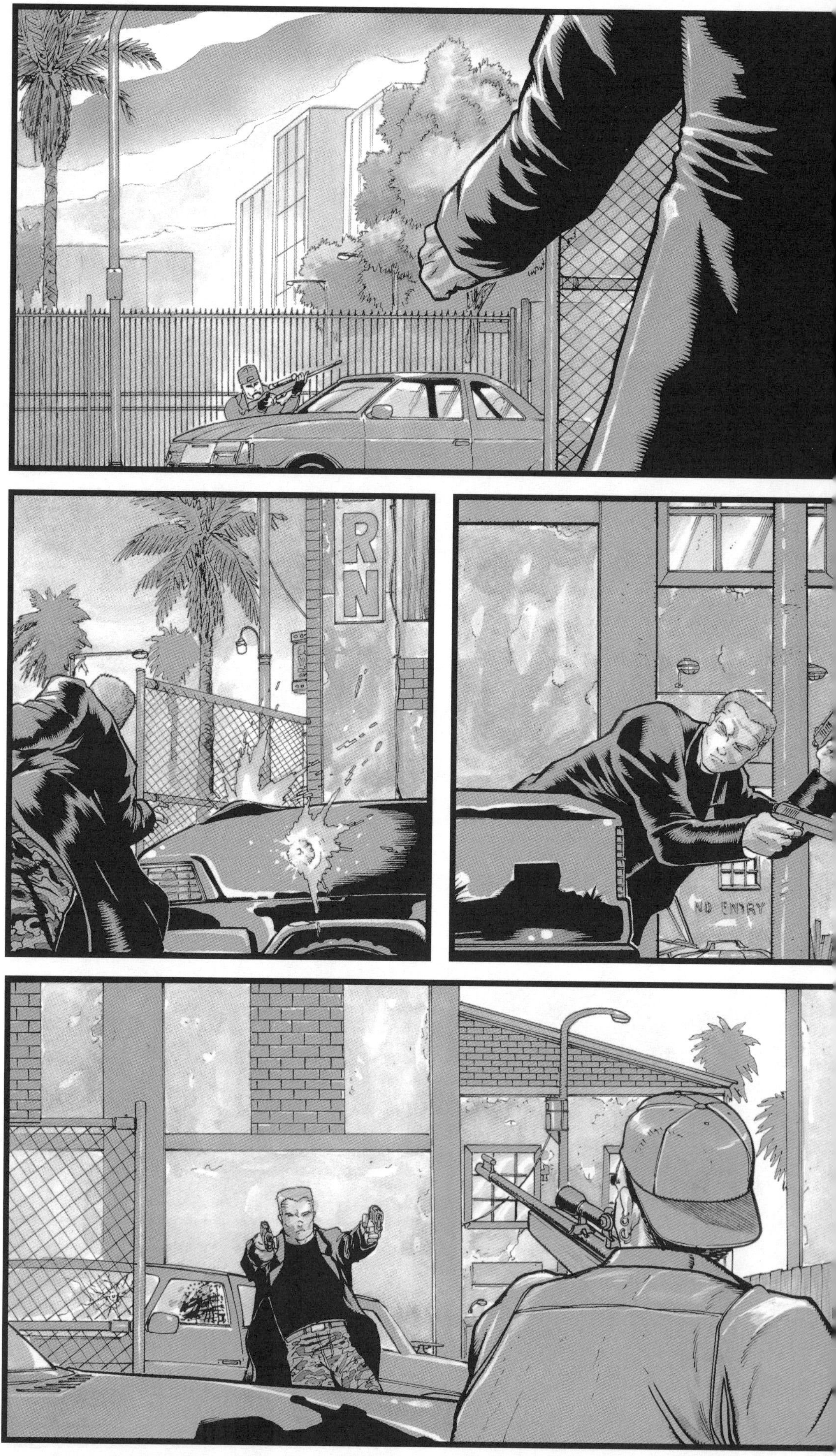
RN
NO ENTRY

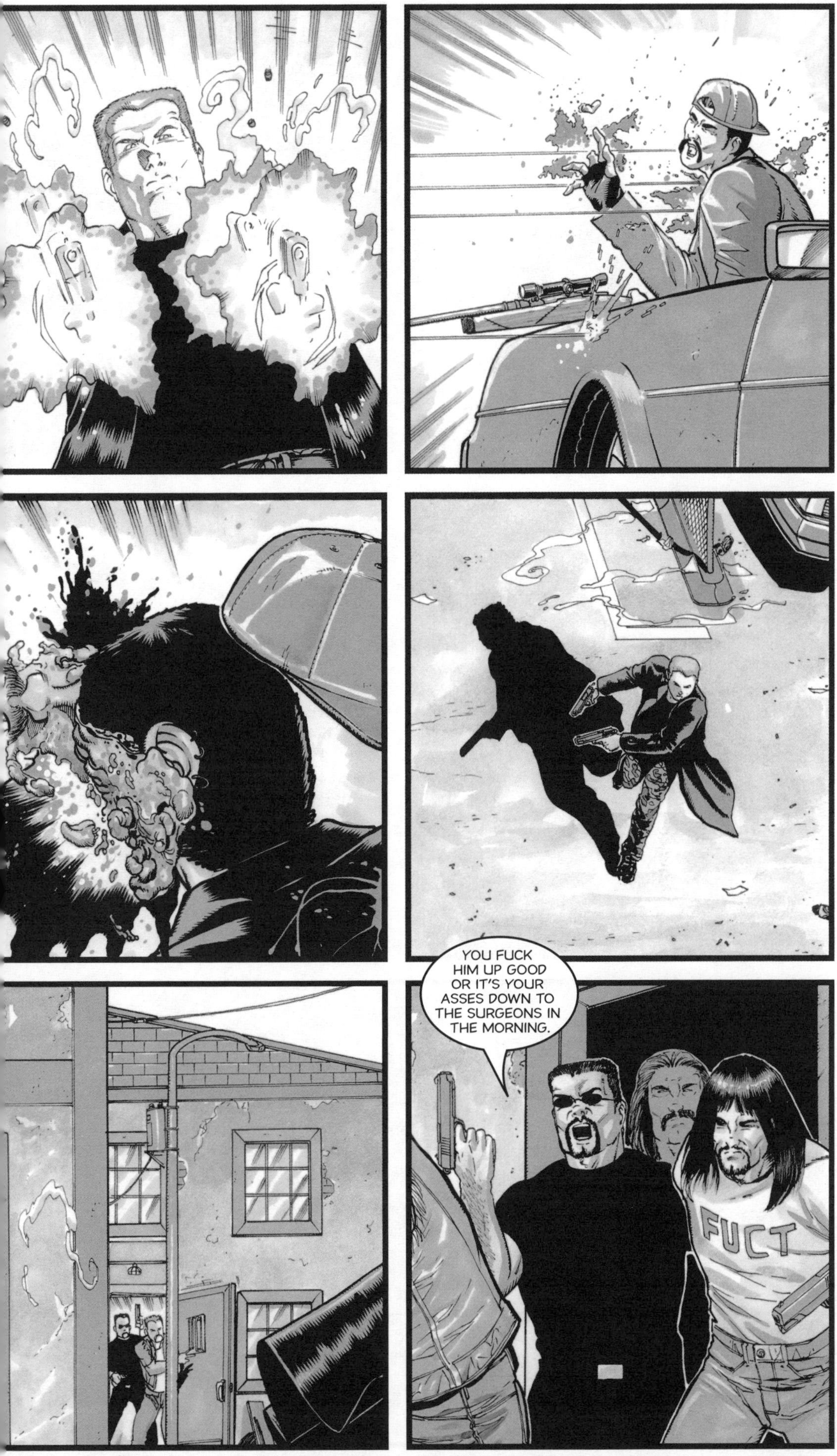
YOU FUCK HIM UP GOOD OR IT'S YOUR ASSES DOWN TO THE SURGEONS IN THE MORNING.
FUCT

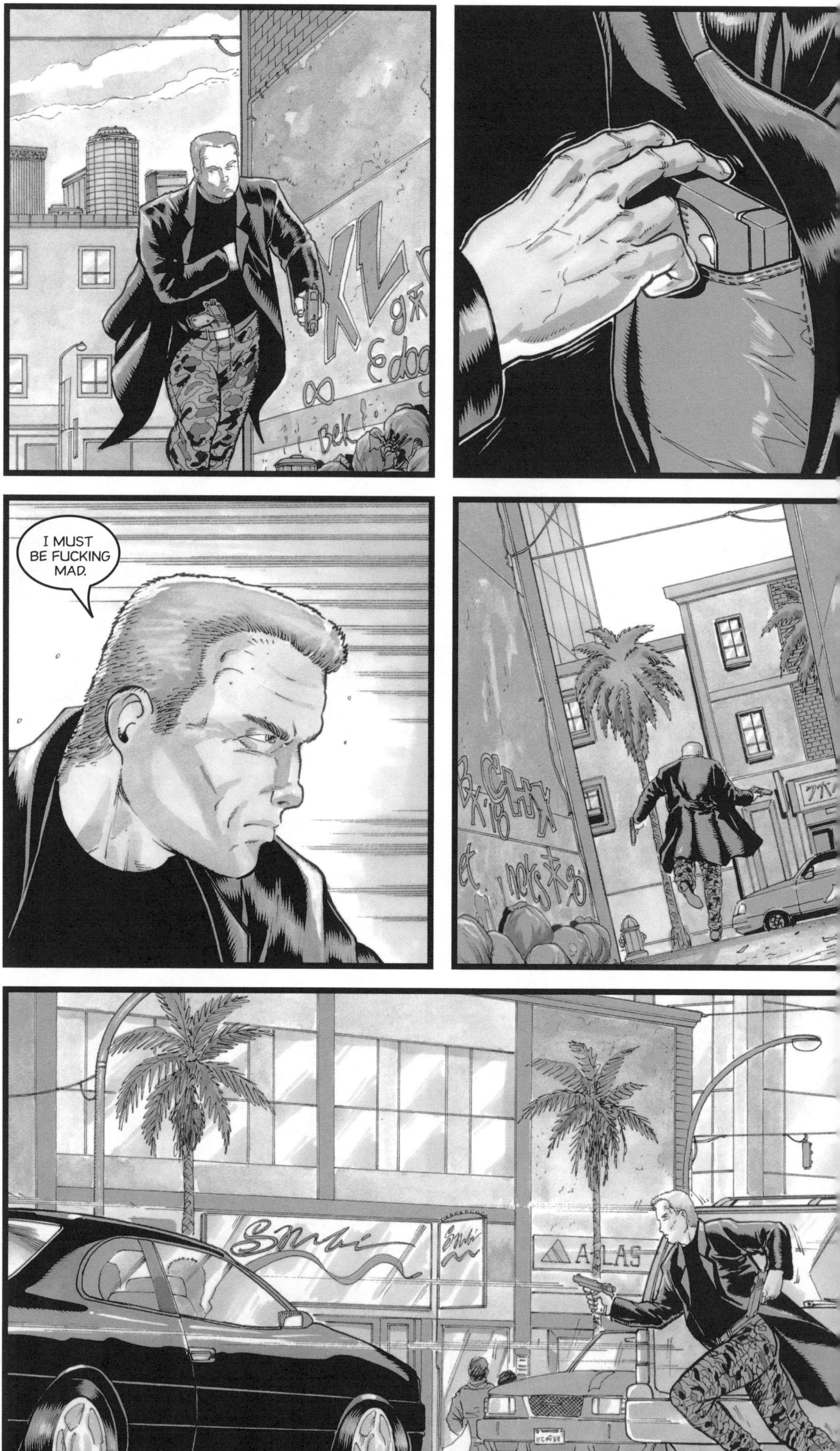
I MUST BE FUCKING MAD.
A-LAS

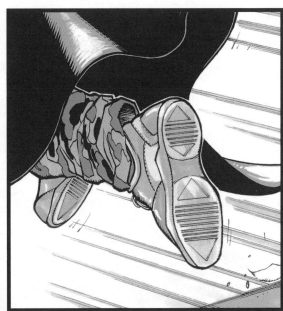

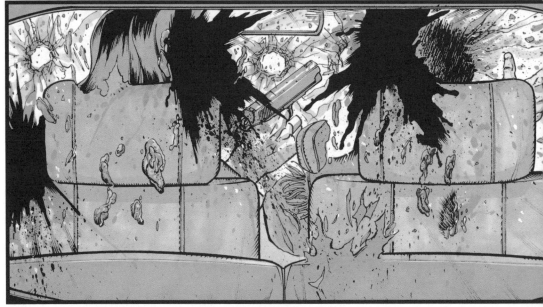

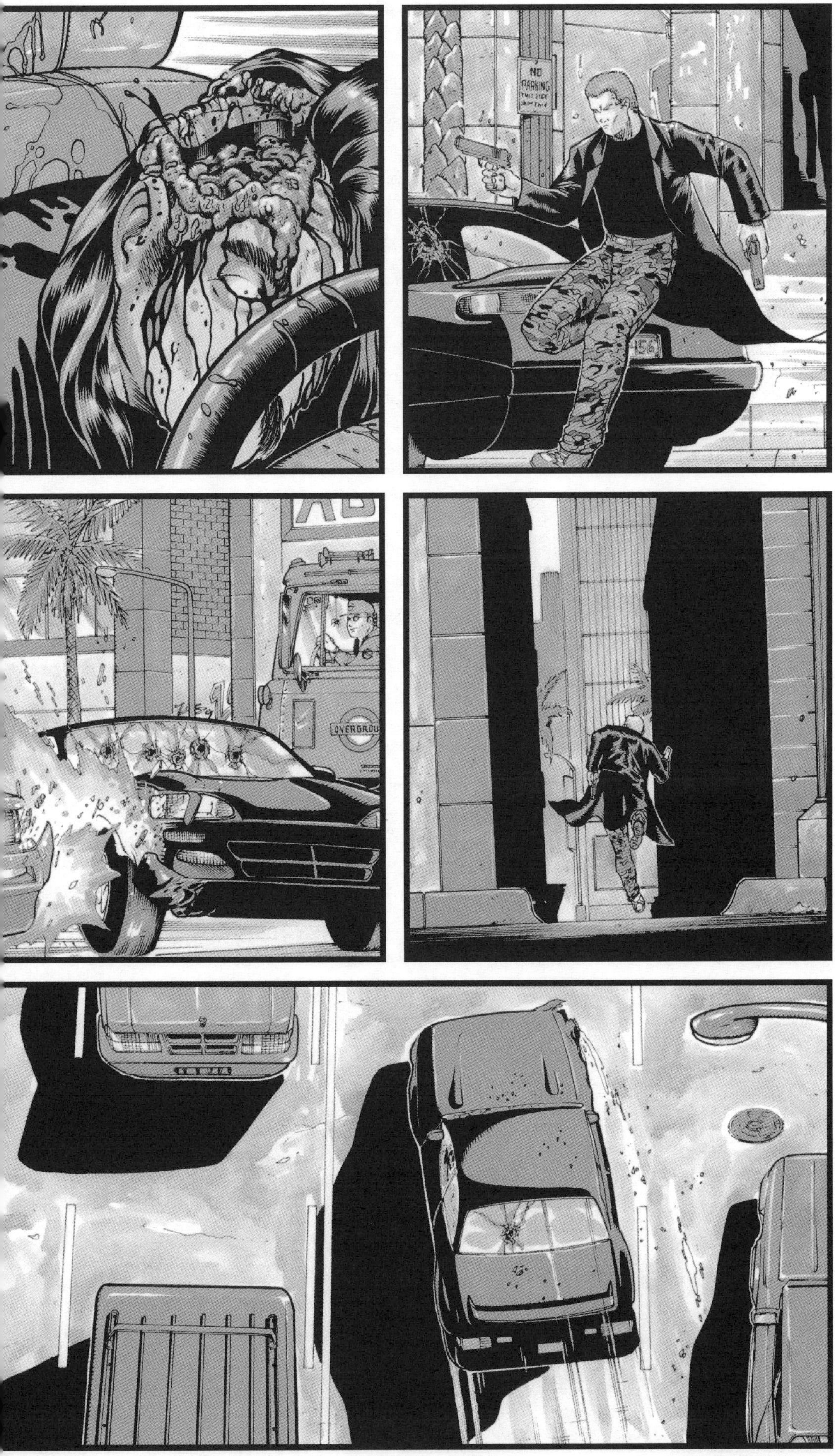
NO PARKING

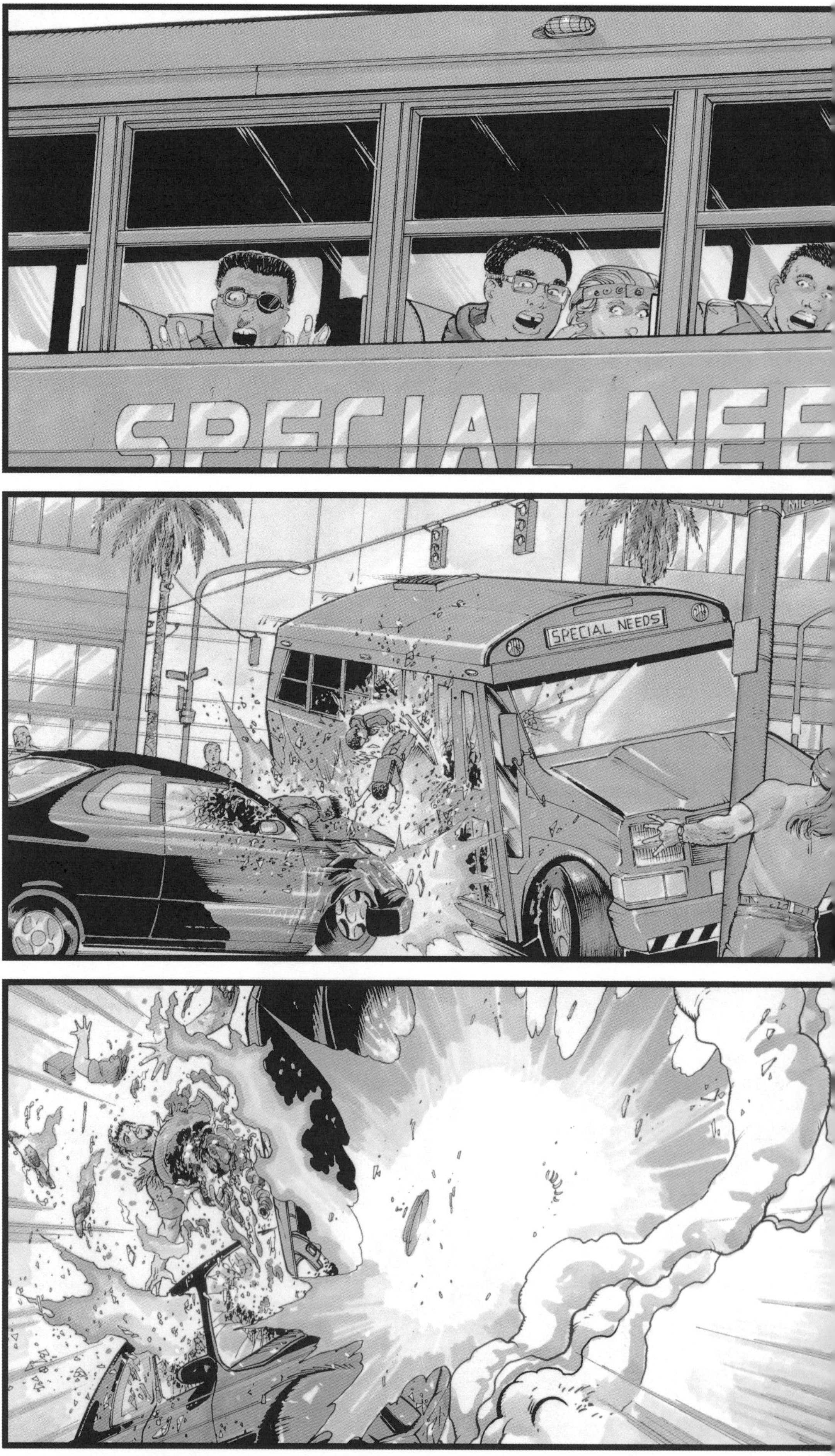
SPECIAL NEE
SPECIAL NEEDS

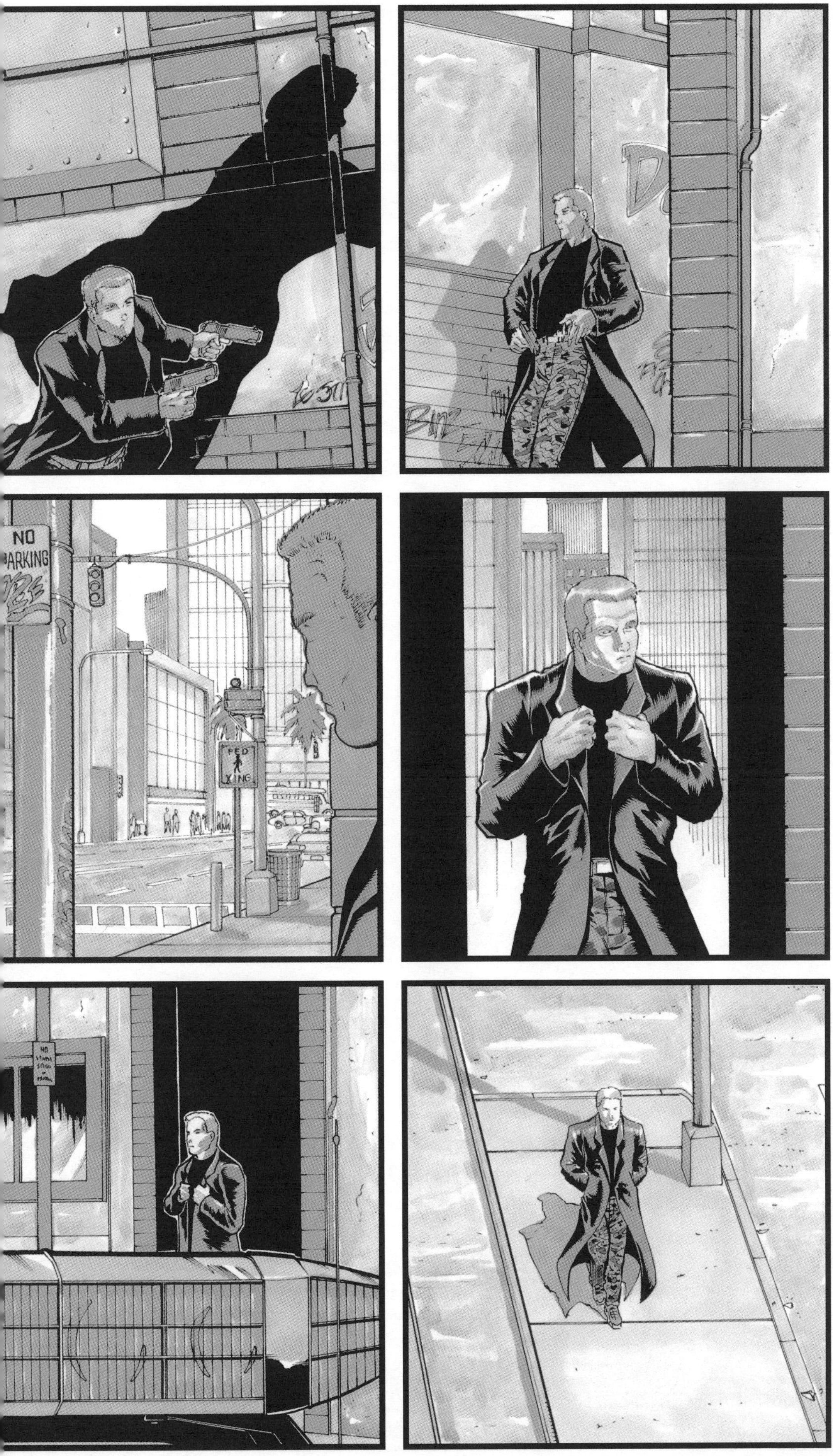
NO PARKING
PED XING

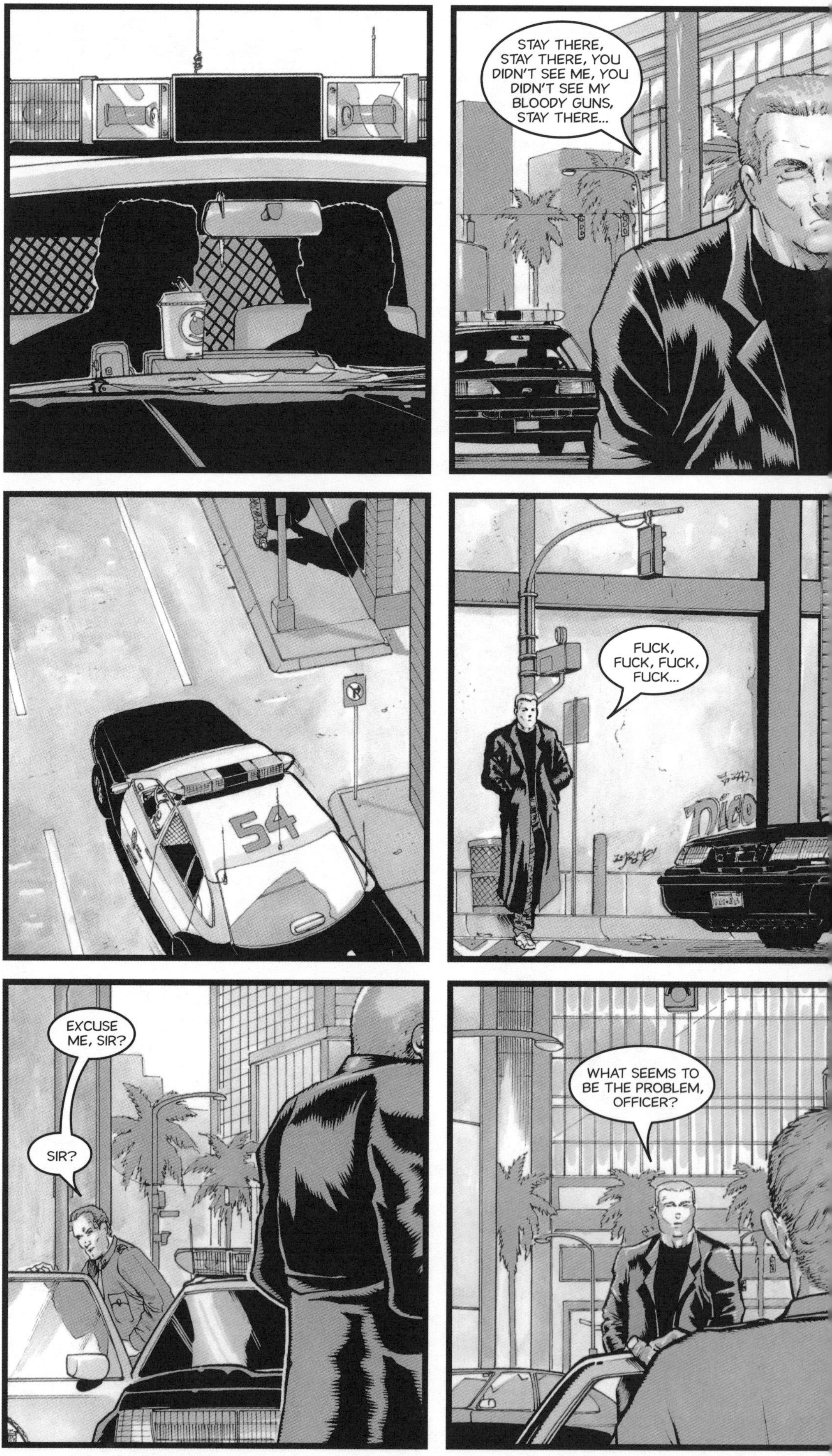
STAY THERE, STAY THERE, YOU DIDN'T SEE ME, YOU DIDN'T SEE MY BLOODY GUNS, STAY THERE...
FUCK, FUCK, FUCK, FUCK...
EXCUSE ME, SIR?
SIR?
WHAT SEEMS TO BE THE PROBLEM, OFFICER?

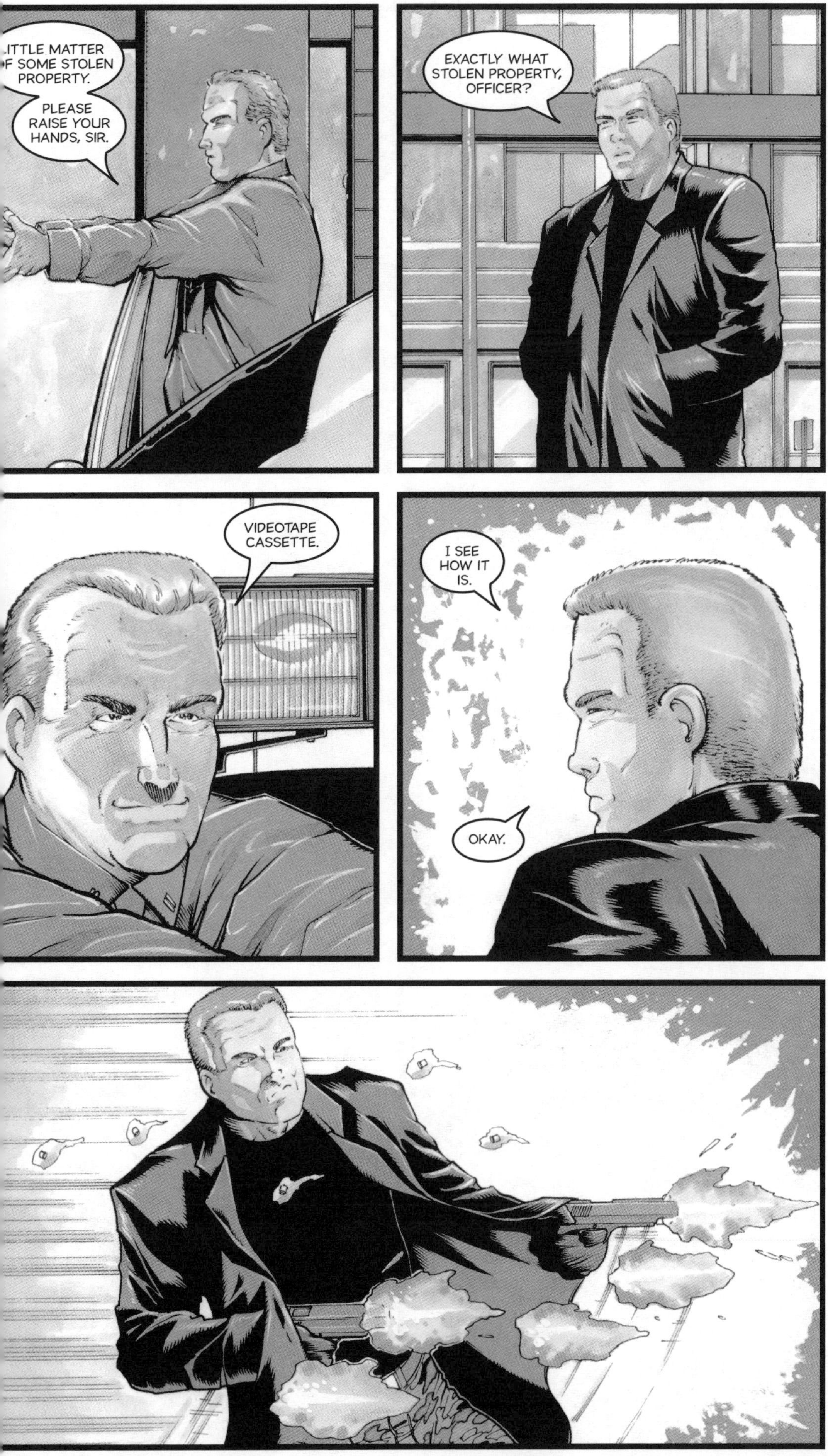

...LITTLE MATTER OF SOME STOLEN PROPERTY.
PLEASE RAISE YOUR HANDS, SIR.
EXACTLY WHAT STOLEN PROPERTY, OFFICER?
VIDEOTAPE CASSETTE.
I SEE HOW IT IS.
OKAY.

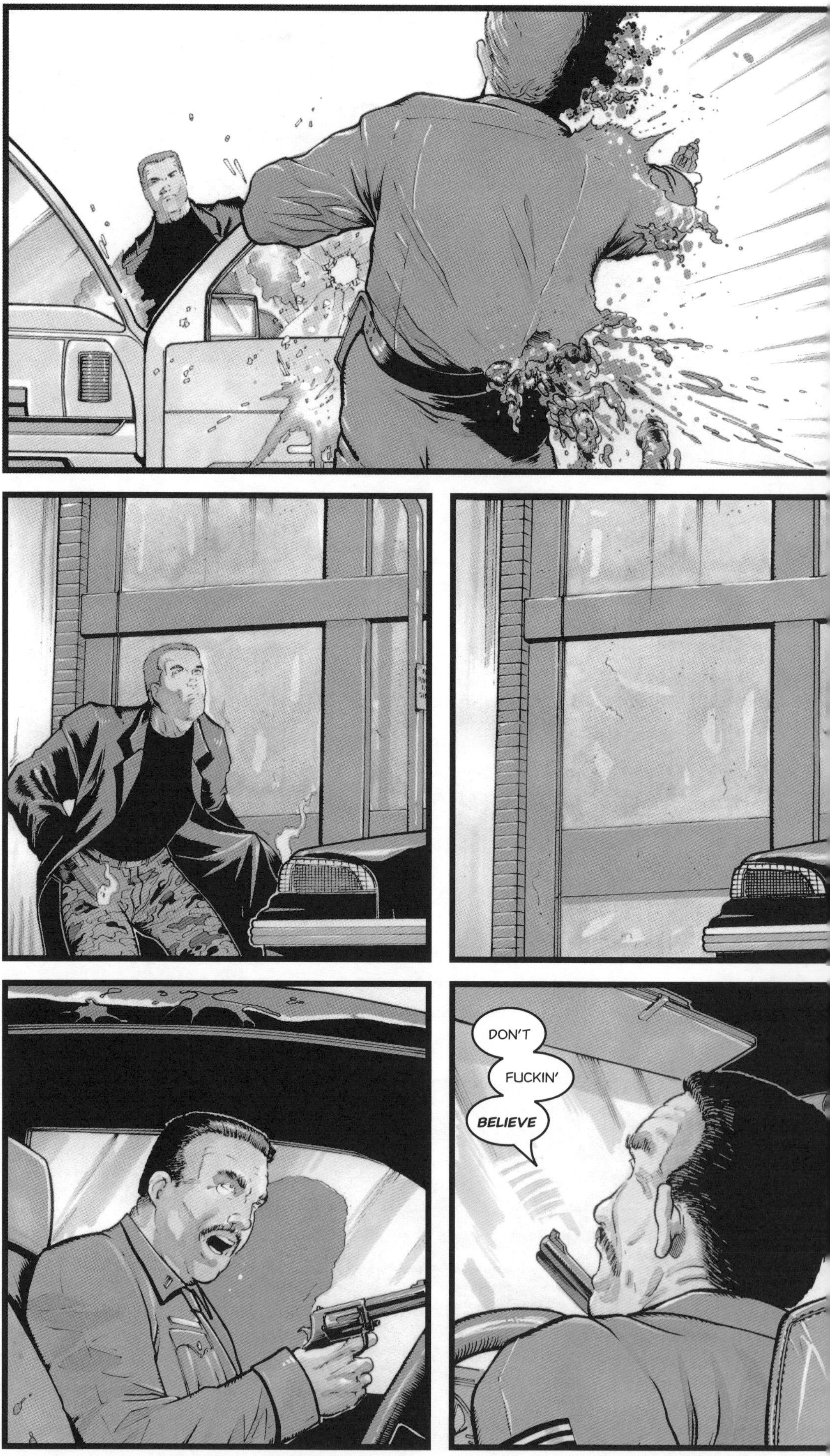
DON'T
FUCKIN'
BELIEVE

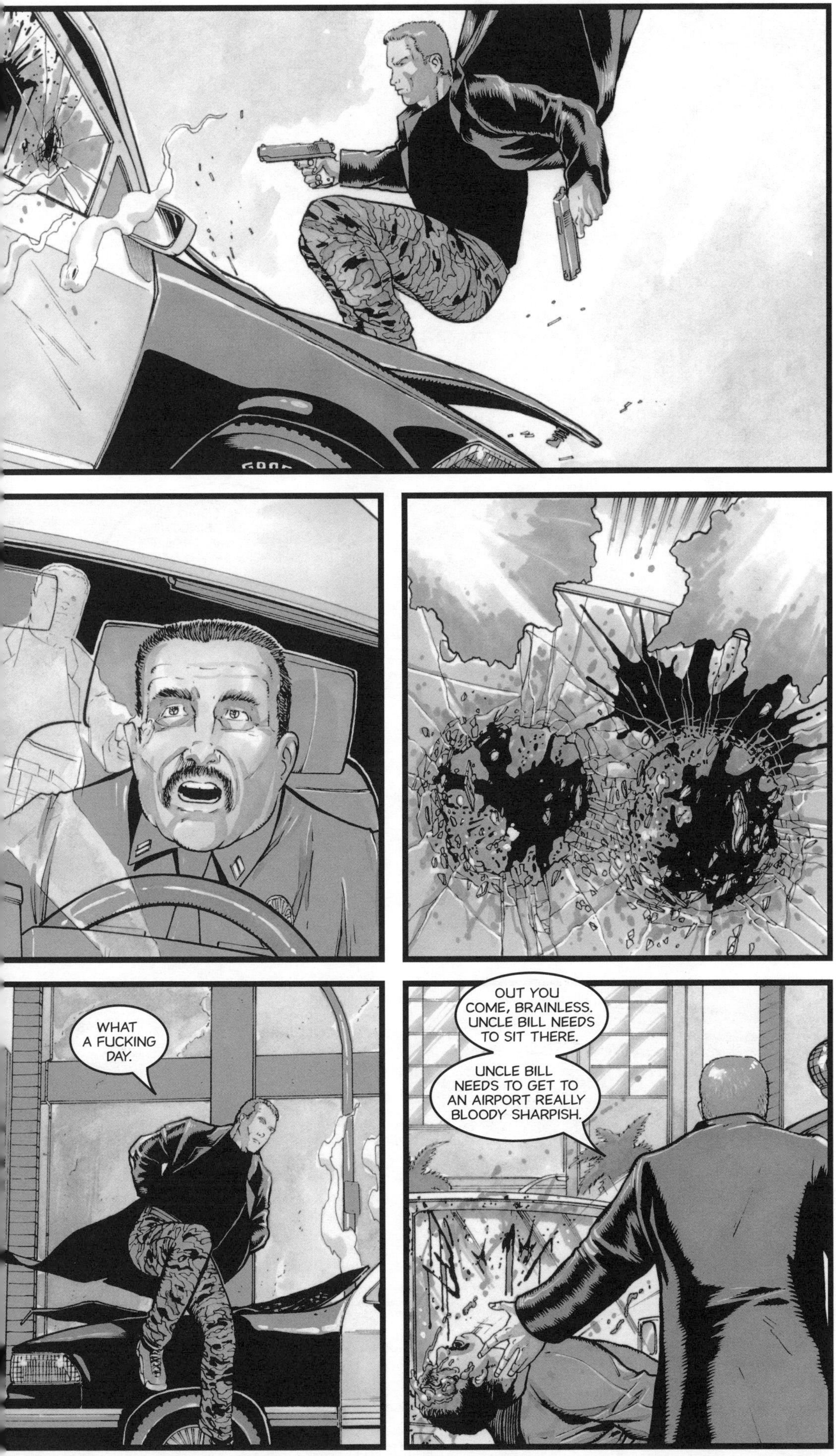

WHAT A FUCKING DAY.
OUT YOU COME, BRAINLESS. UNCLE BILL NEEDS TO SIT THERE.
UNCLE BILL NEEDS TO GET TO AN AIRPORT REALLY BLOODY SHARPISH.

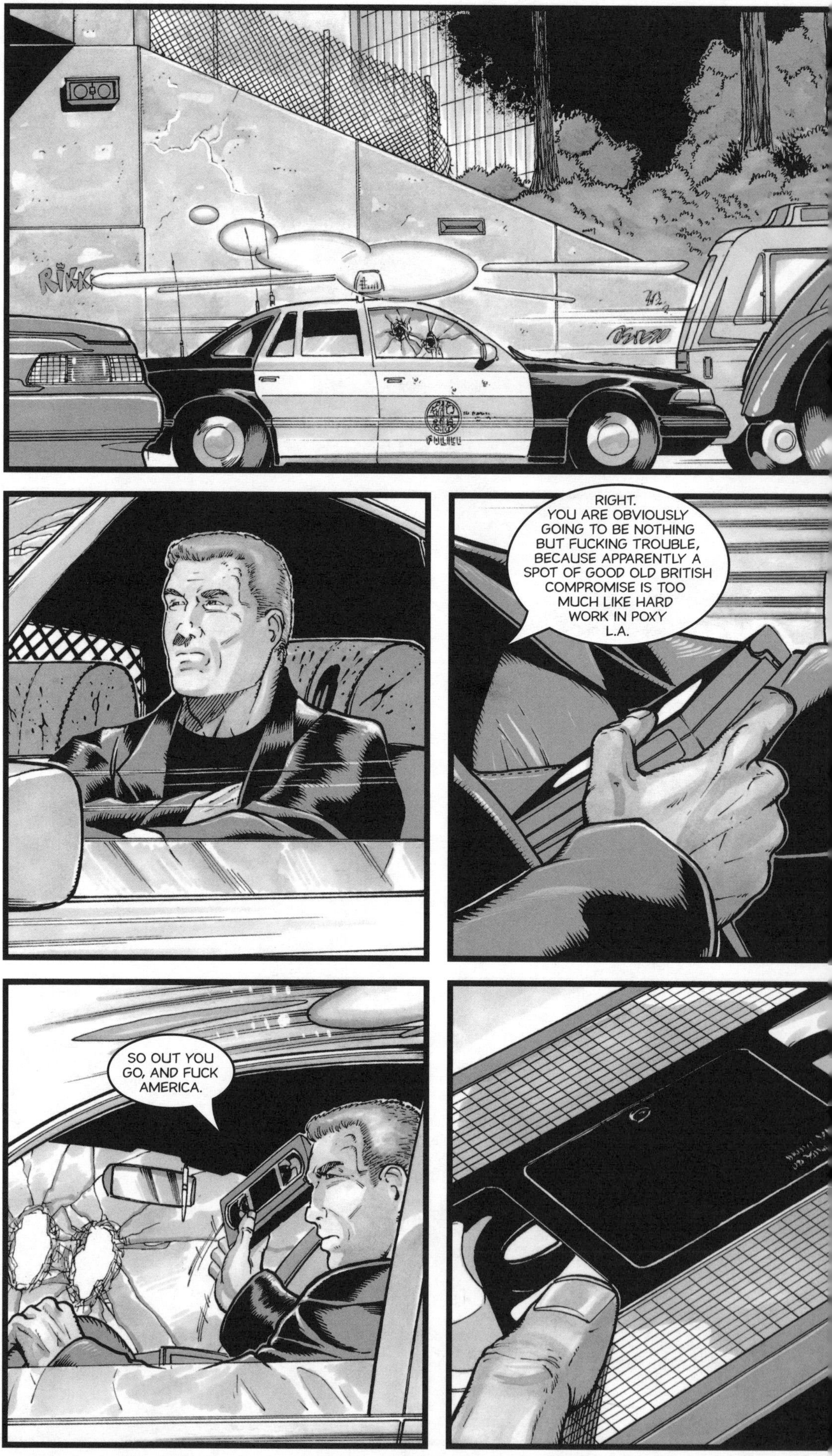
RIGHT. YOU ARE OBVIOUSLY GOING TO BE NOTHING BUT FUCKING TROUBLE, BECAUSE APPARENTLY A SPOT OF GOOD OLD BRITISH COMPROMISE IS TOO MUCH LIKE HARD WORK IN POXY L.A.
SO OUT YOU GO, AND FUCK AMERICA.

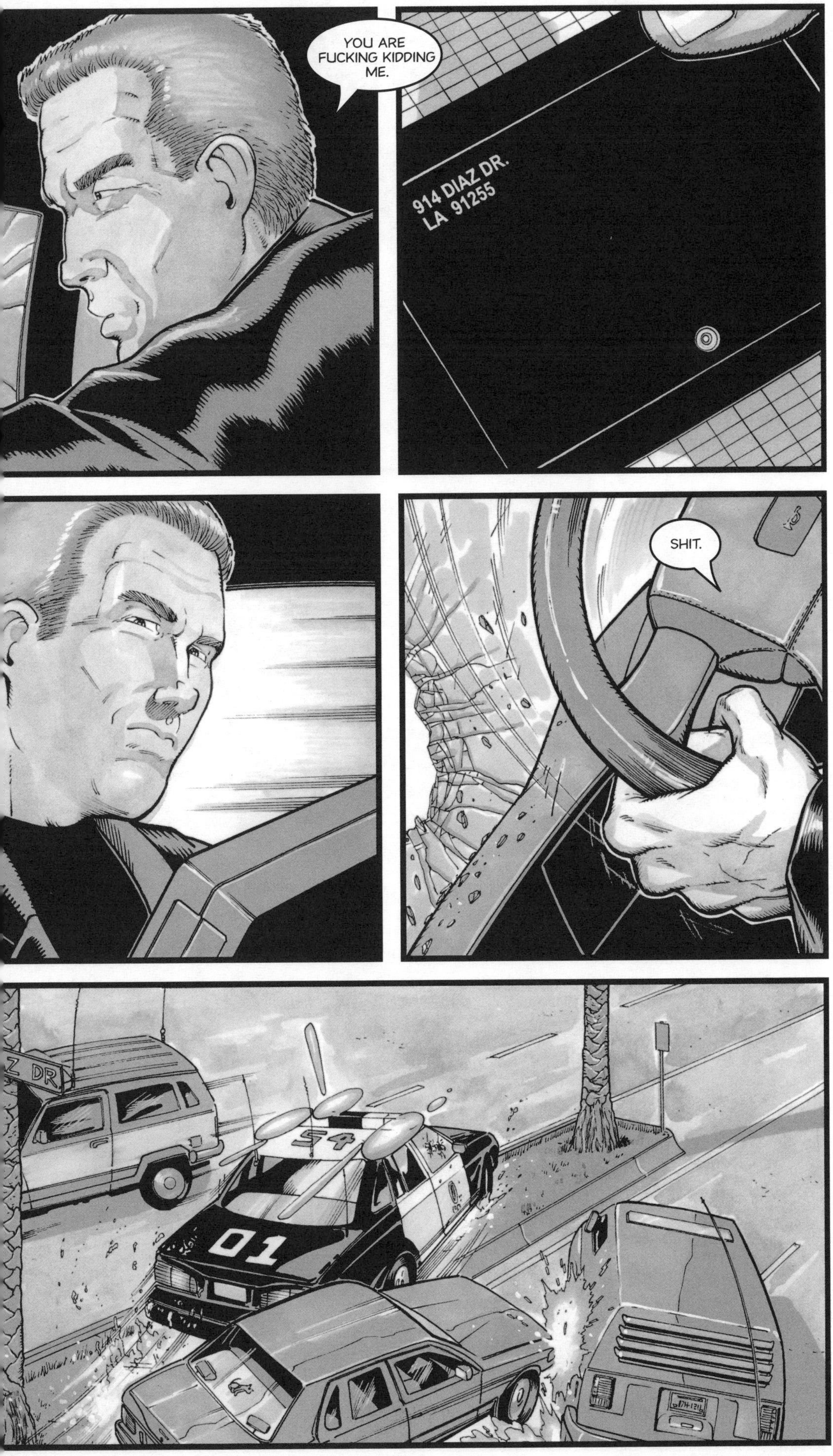
YOU ARE FUCKING KIDDING ME.
914 DIAZ DR.
LA 91255
SHIT.
Z DR
54
01

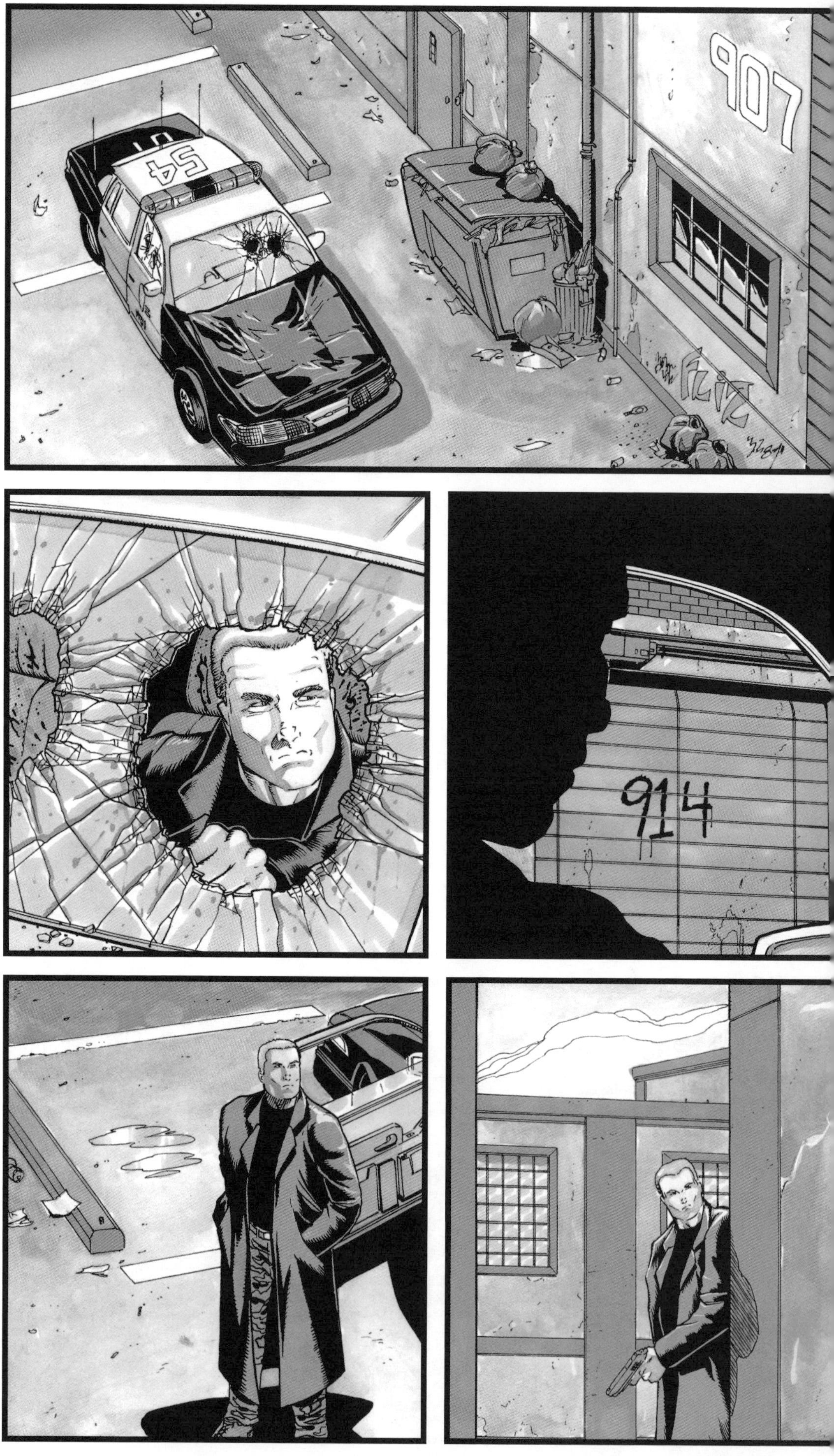
907
54
914

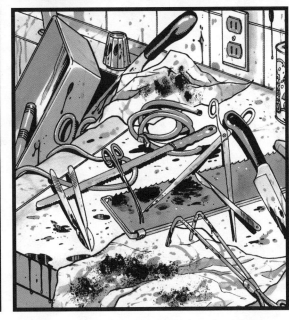

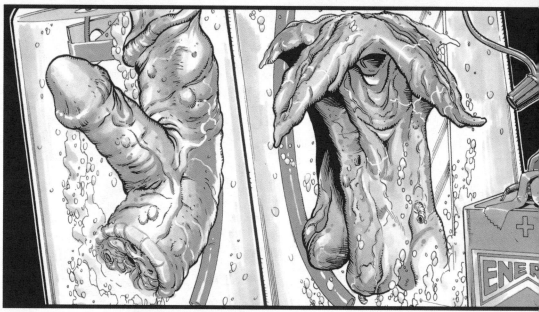

IT'S THE SURGERY.

HELLO.

stranger kisses ™

THREE

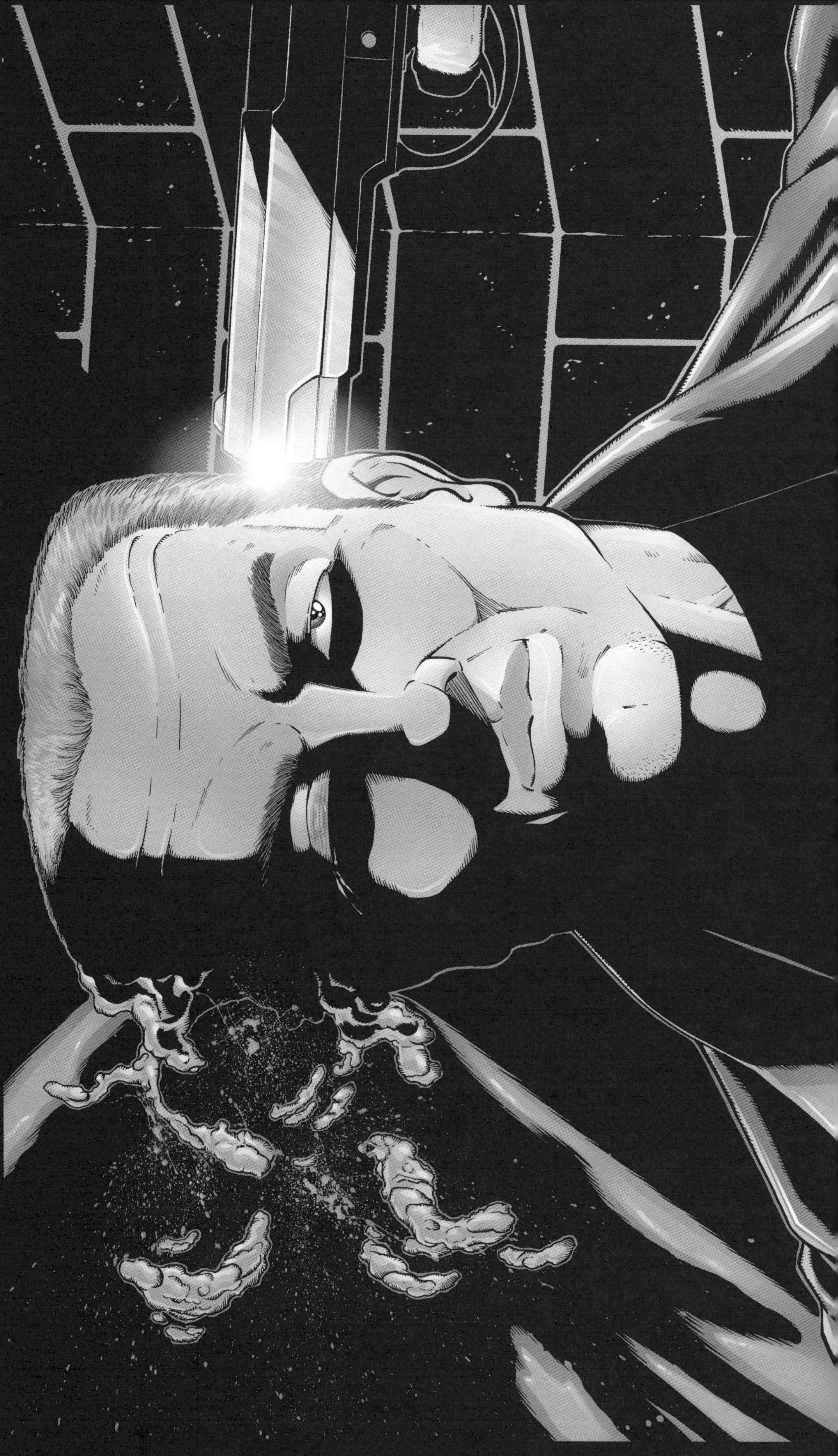

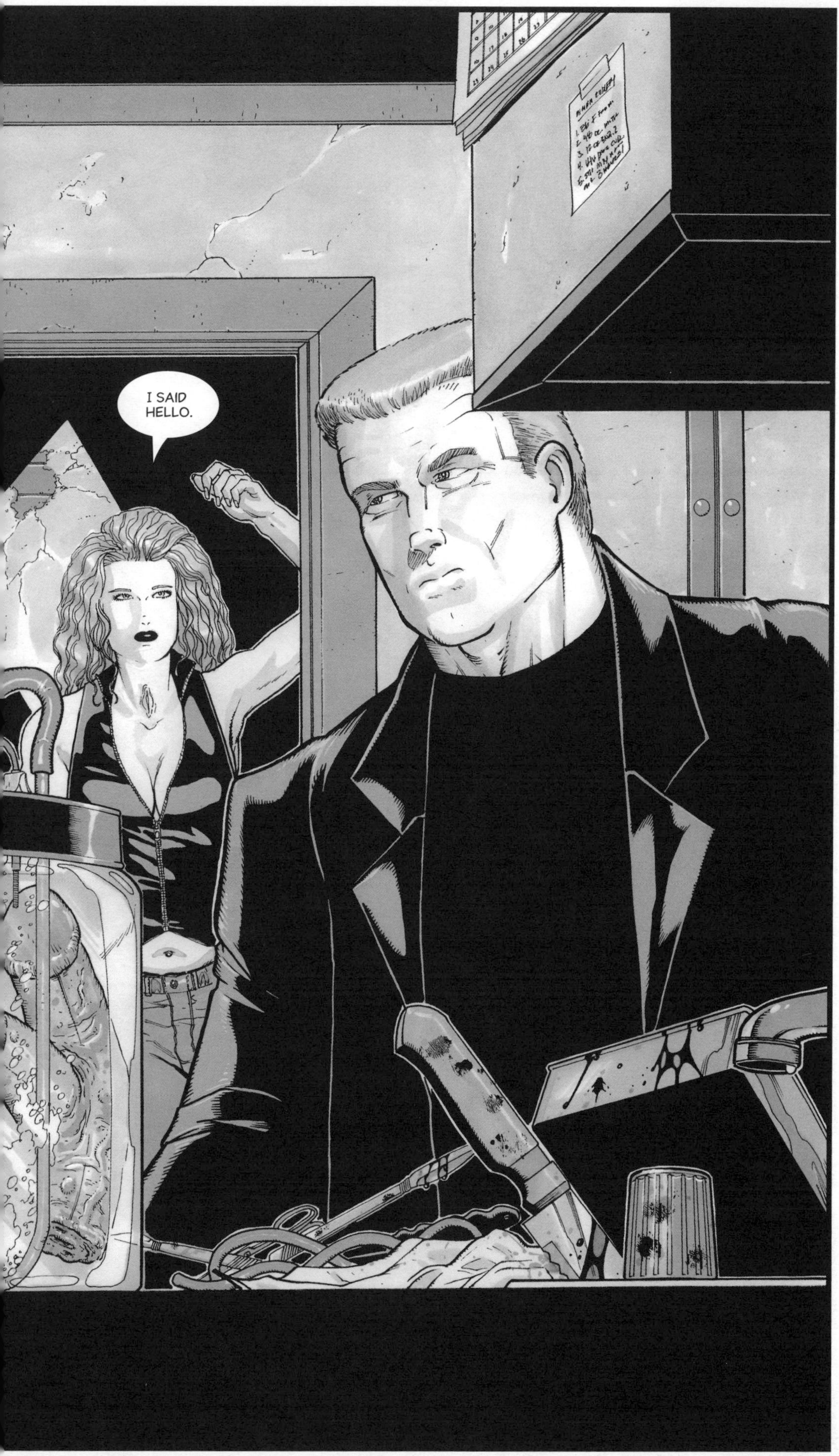
I SAID HELLO.

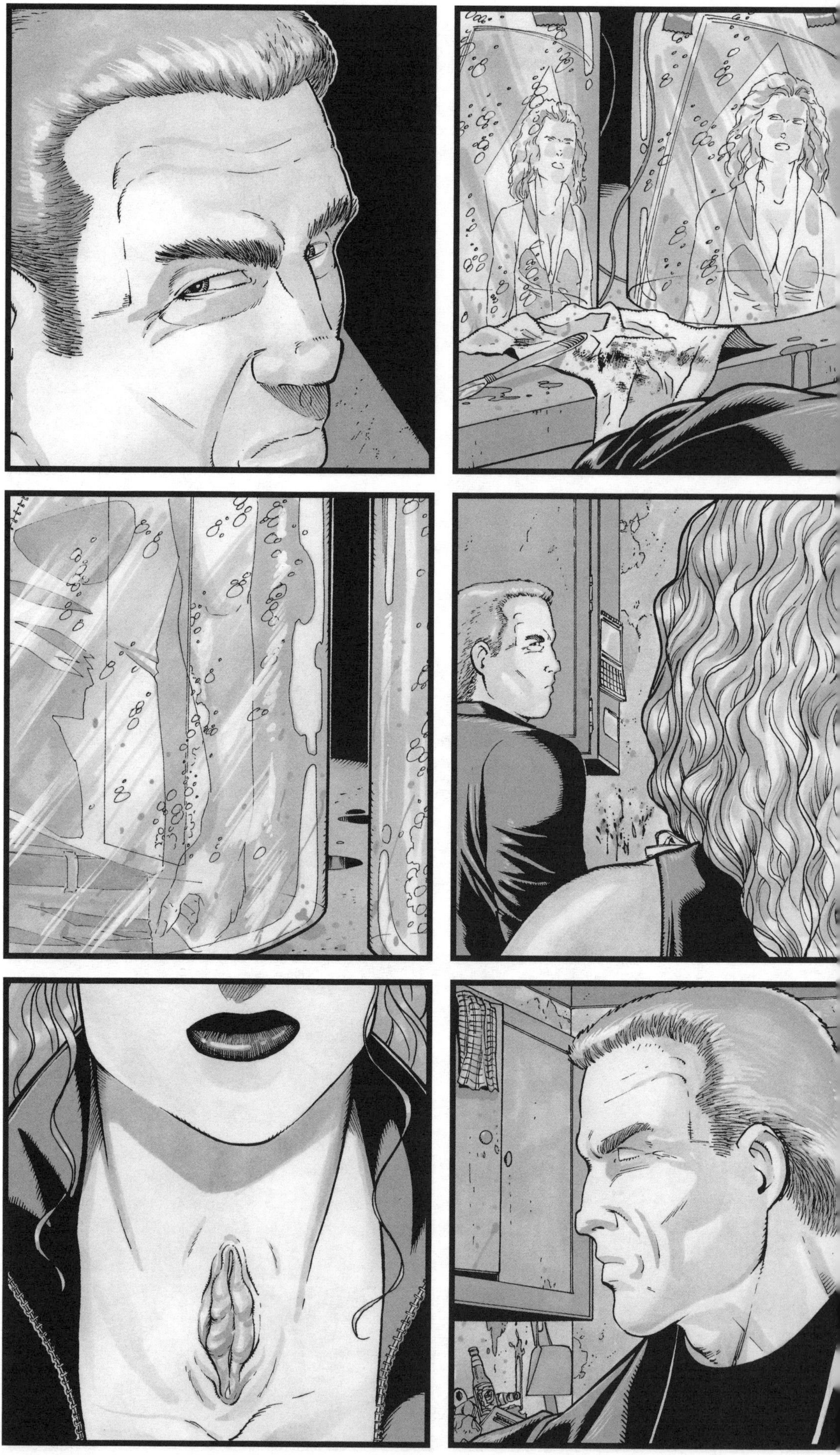

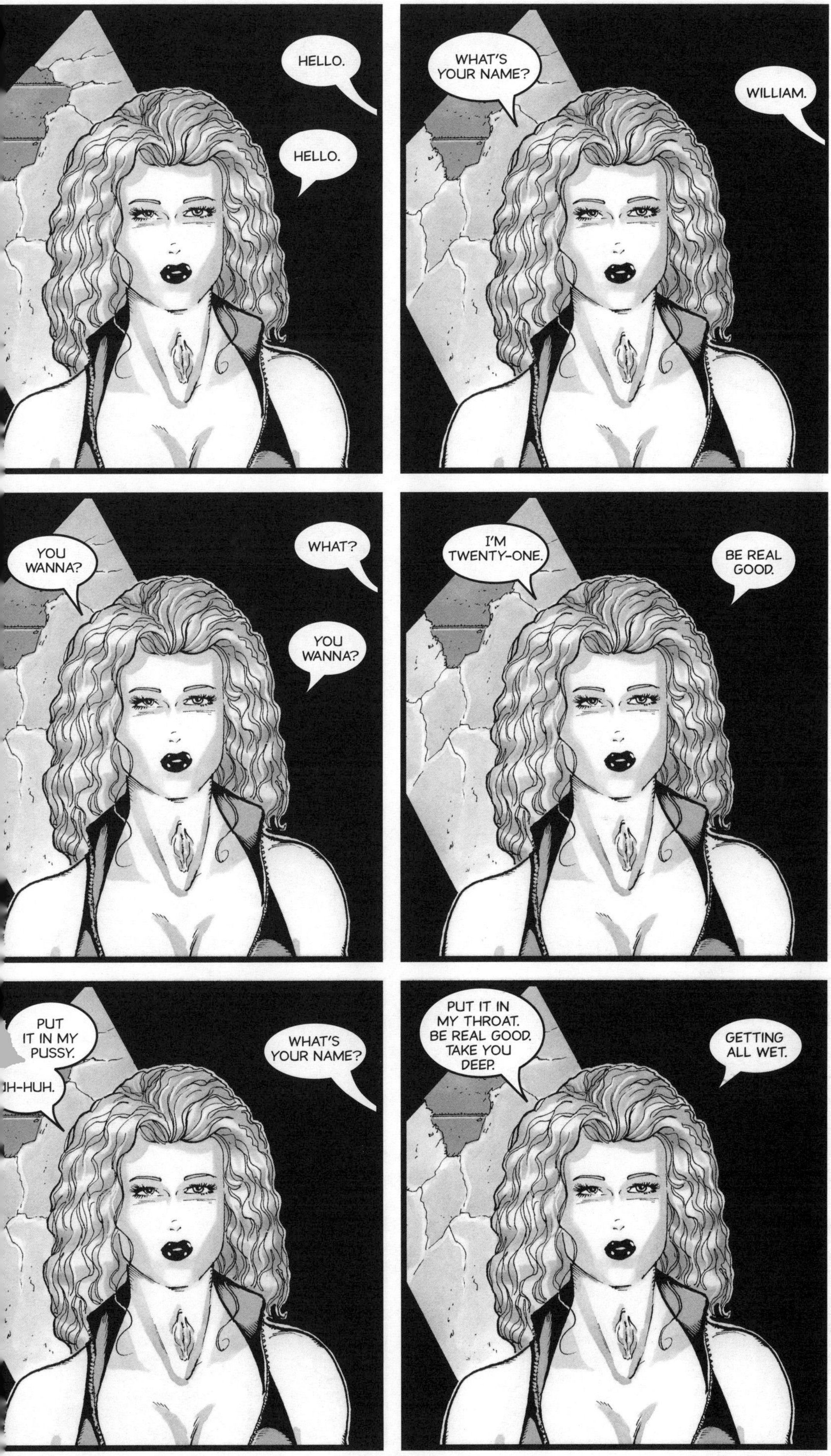
HELLO.
HELLO.
WHAT'S YOUR NAME?
WILLIAM.
YOU WANNA?
WHAT?
YOU WANNA?
I'M TWENTY-ONE.
BE REAL GOOD.
PUT IT IN MY PUSSY.
WHAT'S YOUR NAME?
H-HUH.
PUT IT IN MY THROAT. BE REAL GOOD. TAKE YOU DEEP.
GETTING ALL WET.

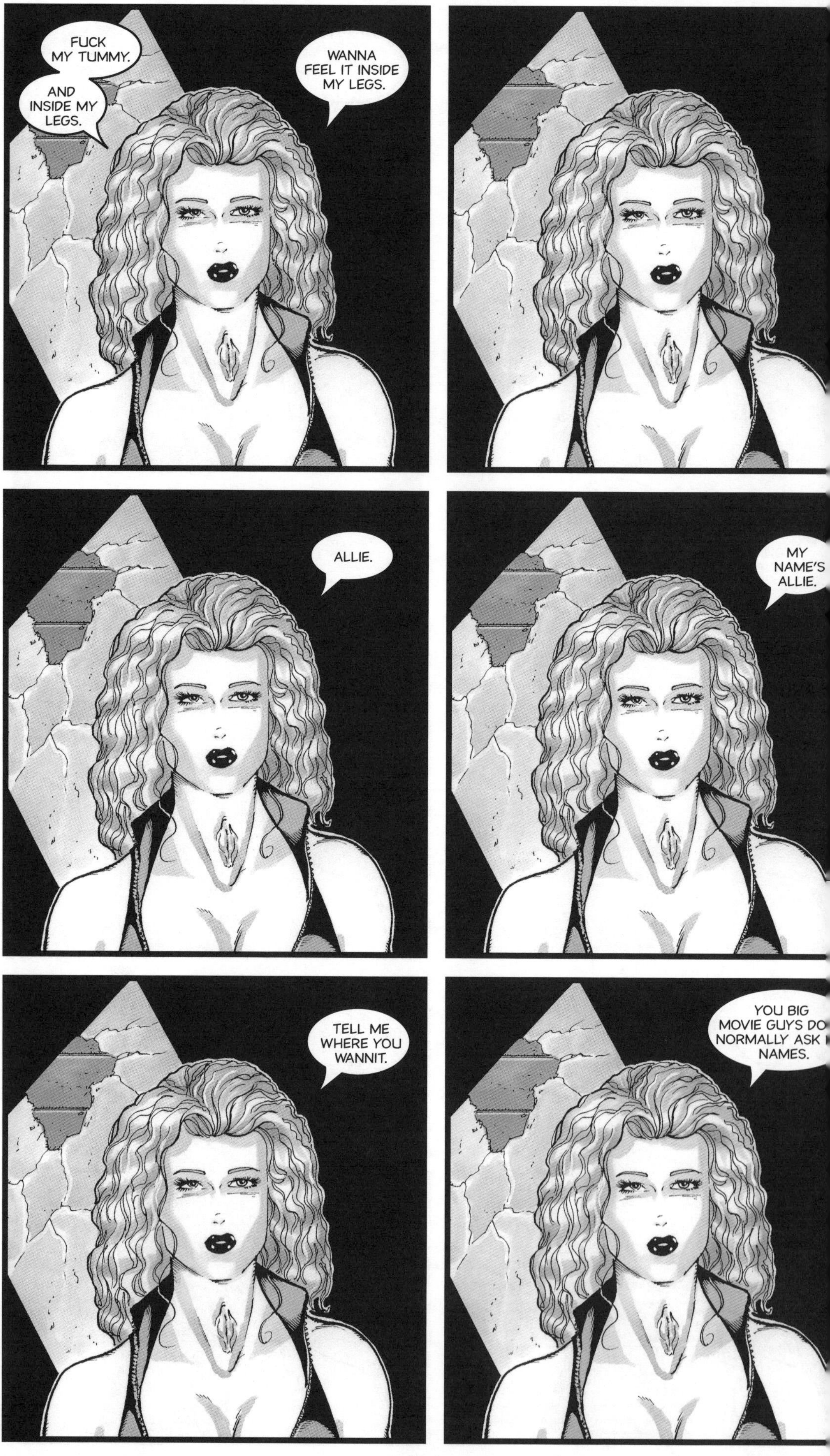
FUCK MY TUMMY.
AND INSIDE MY LEGS.
WANNA FEEL IT INSIDE MY LEGS.
ALLIE.
MY NAME'S ALLIE.
TELL ME WHERE YOU WANNIT.
YOU BIG MOVIE GUYS DO NORMALLY ASK NAMES.

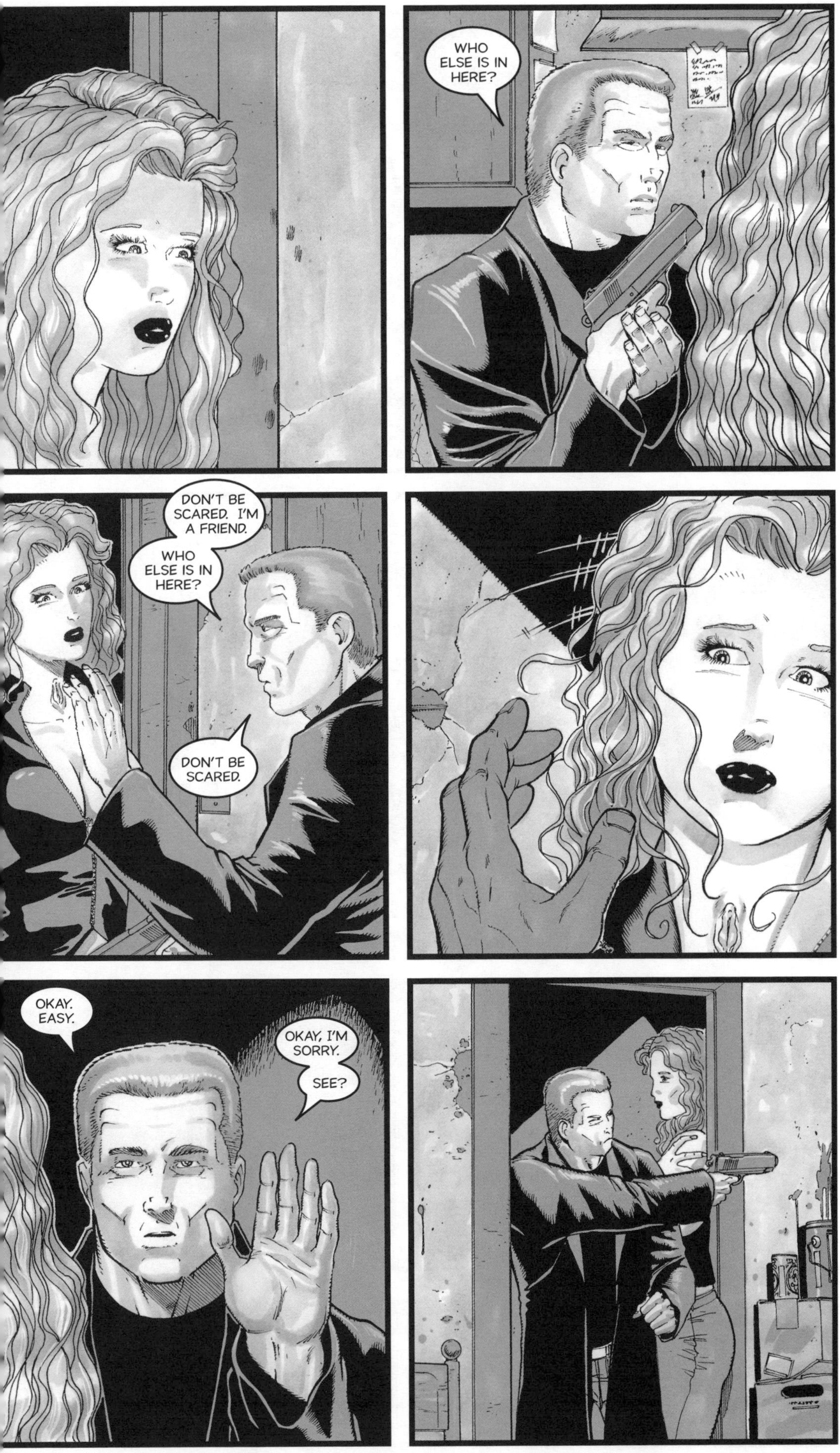
WHO ELSE IS IN HERE?
DON'T BE SCARED. I'M A FRIEND.
WHO ELSE IS IN HERE?
DON'T BE SCARED.
OKAY. EASY.
OKAY, I'M SORRY.
SEE?

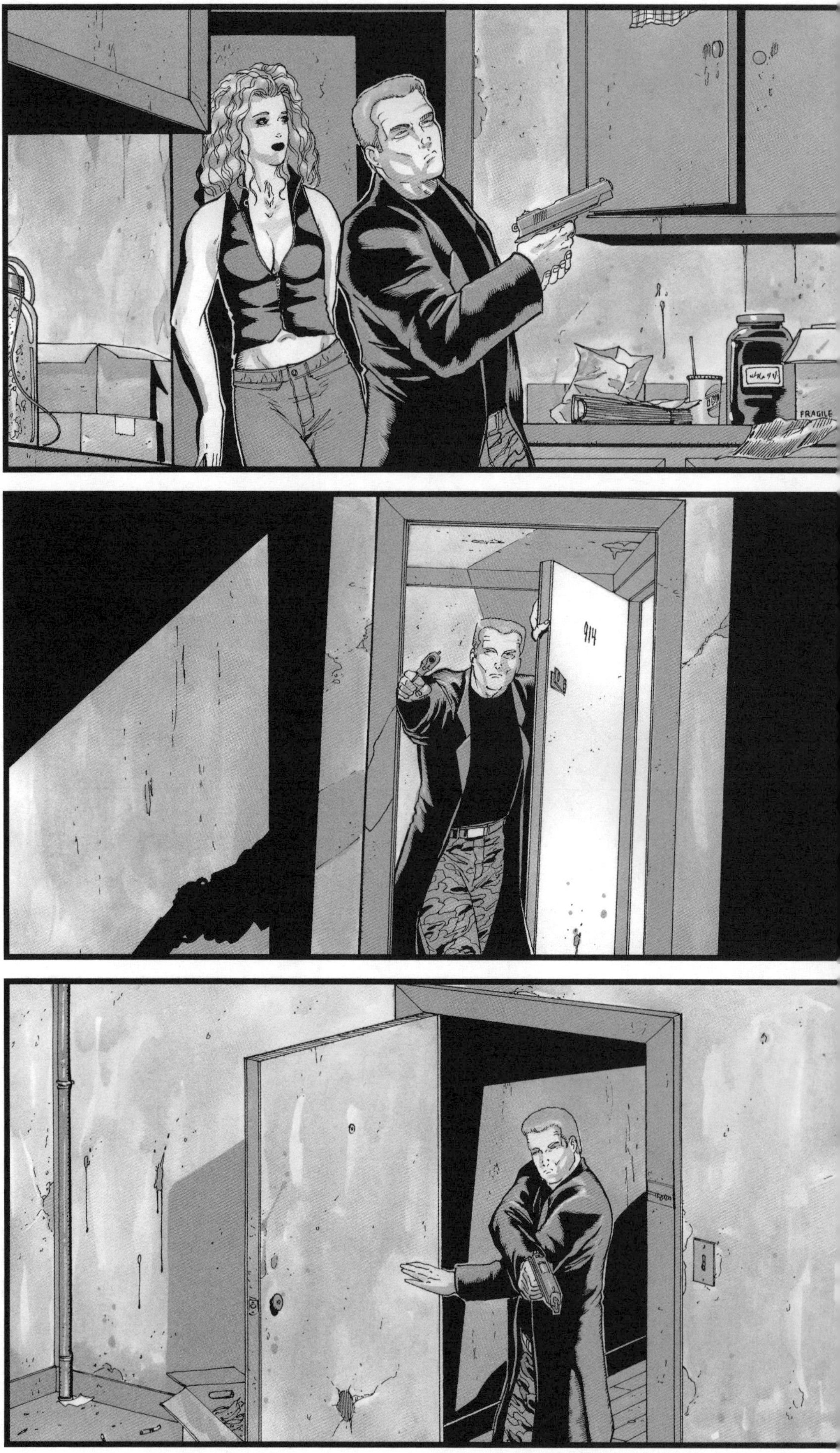
FRAGILE
914

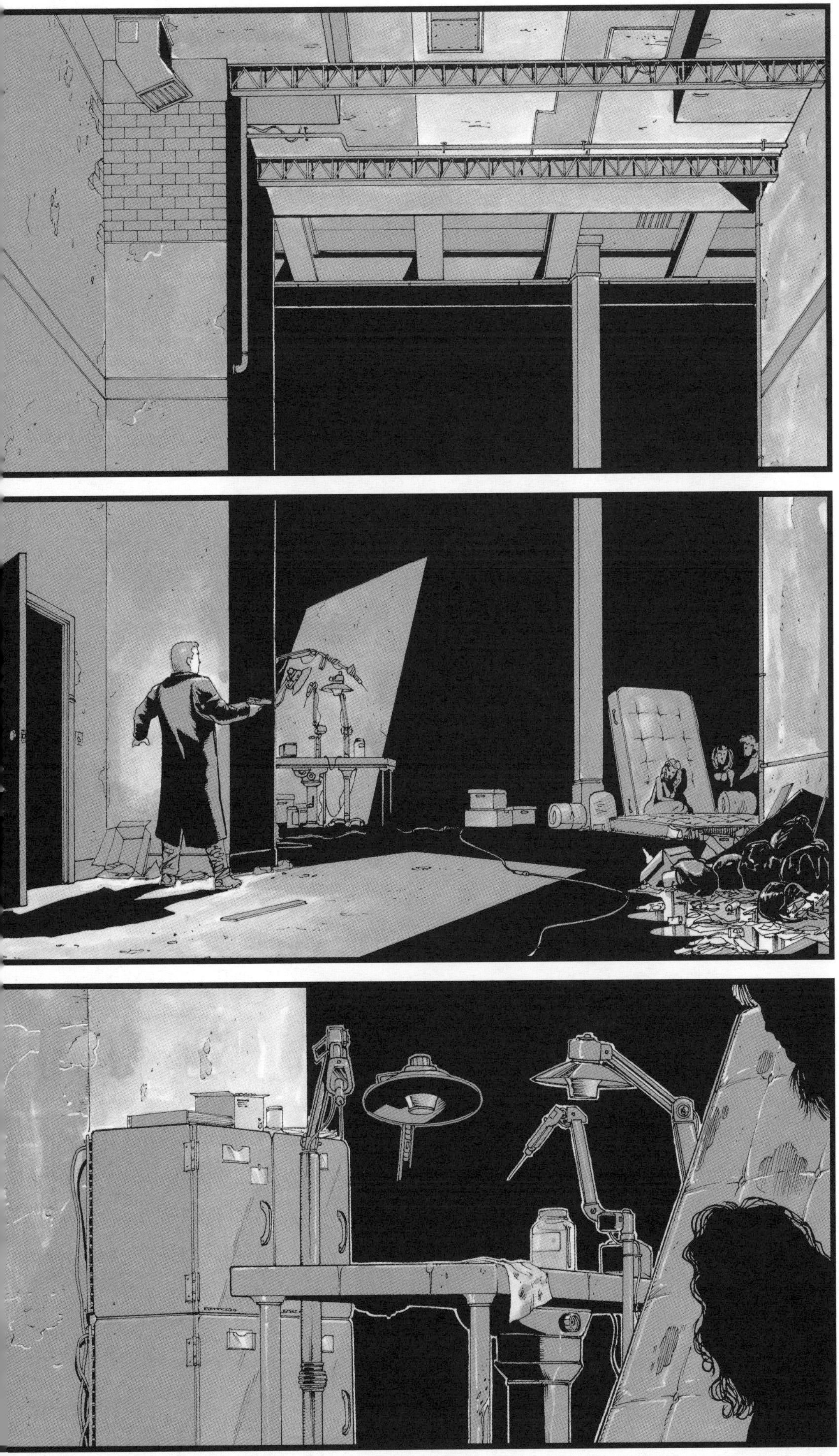

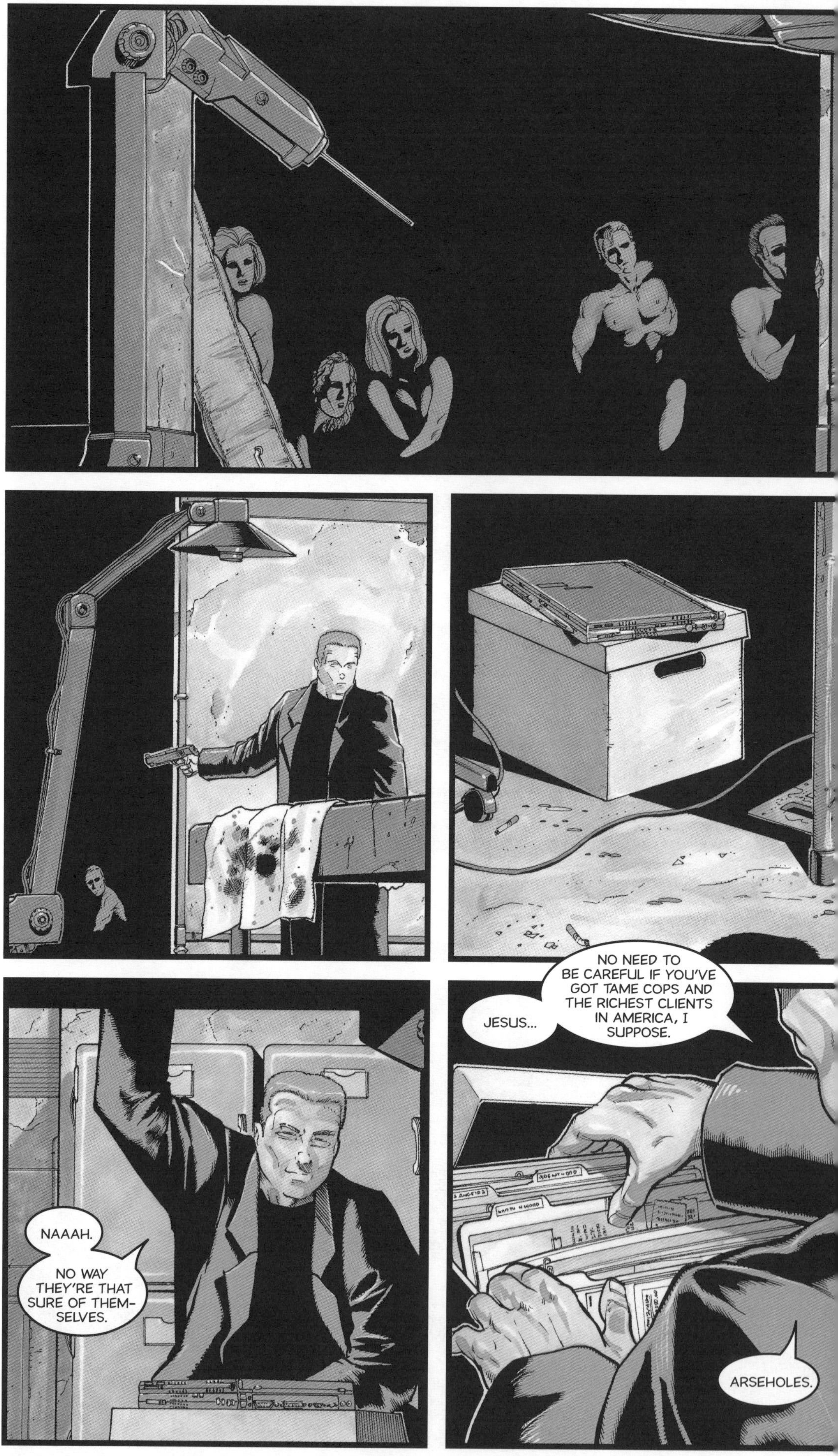
NAAAH.
NO WAY THEY'RE THAT SURE OF THEM-SELVES.
JESUS...
NO NEED TO BE CAREFUL IF YOU'VE GOT TAME COPS AND THE RICHEST CLIENTS IN AMERICA, I SUPPOSE.
ARSEHOLES.

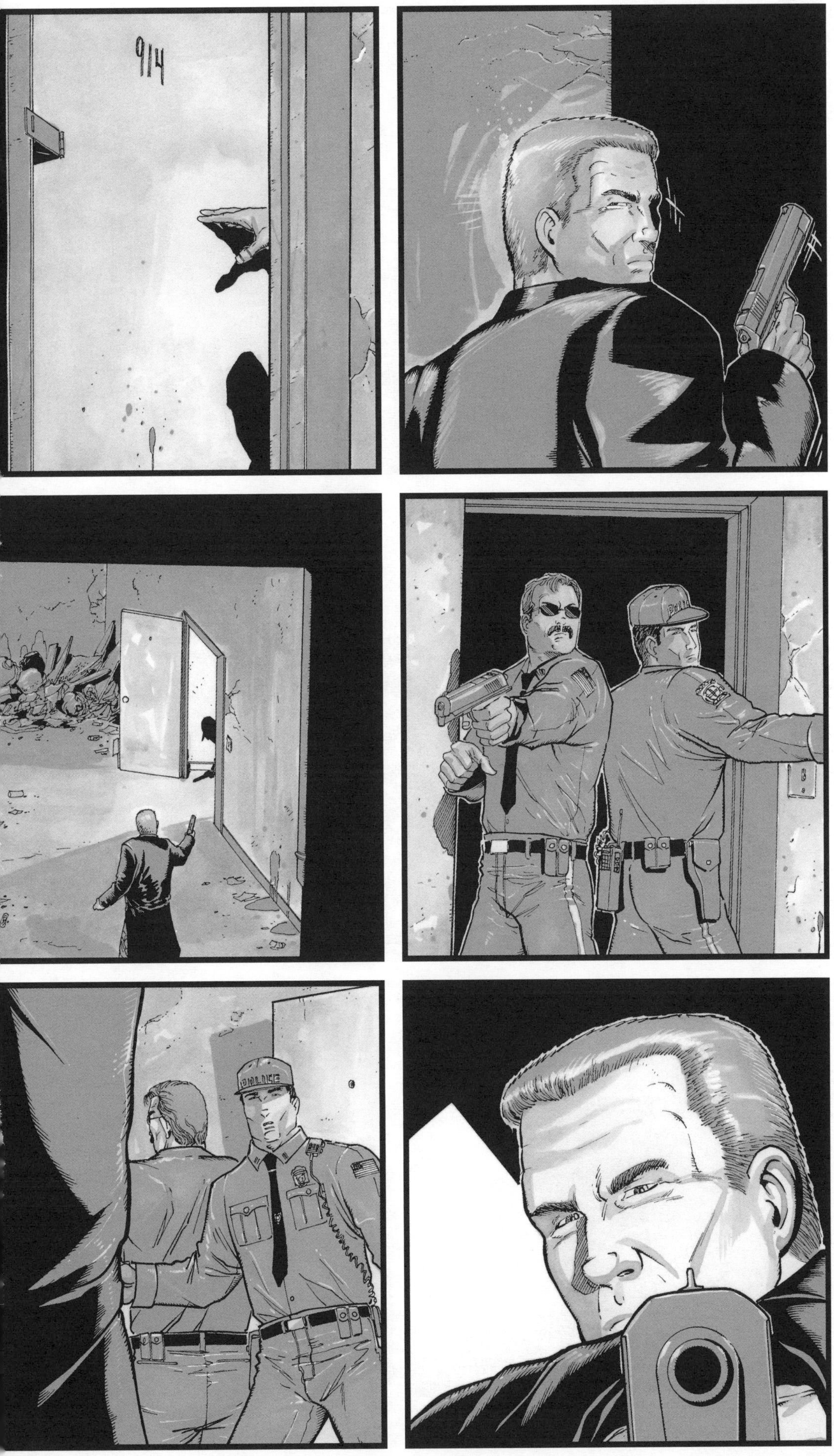
914
POLICE

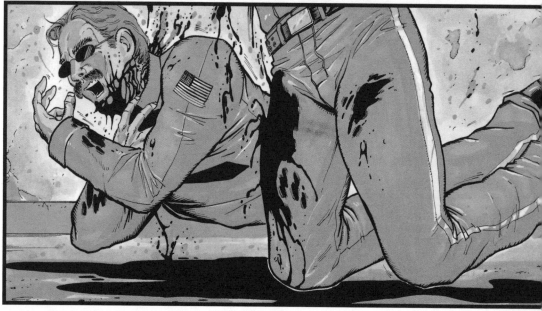

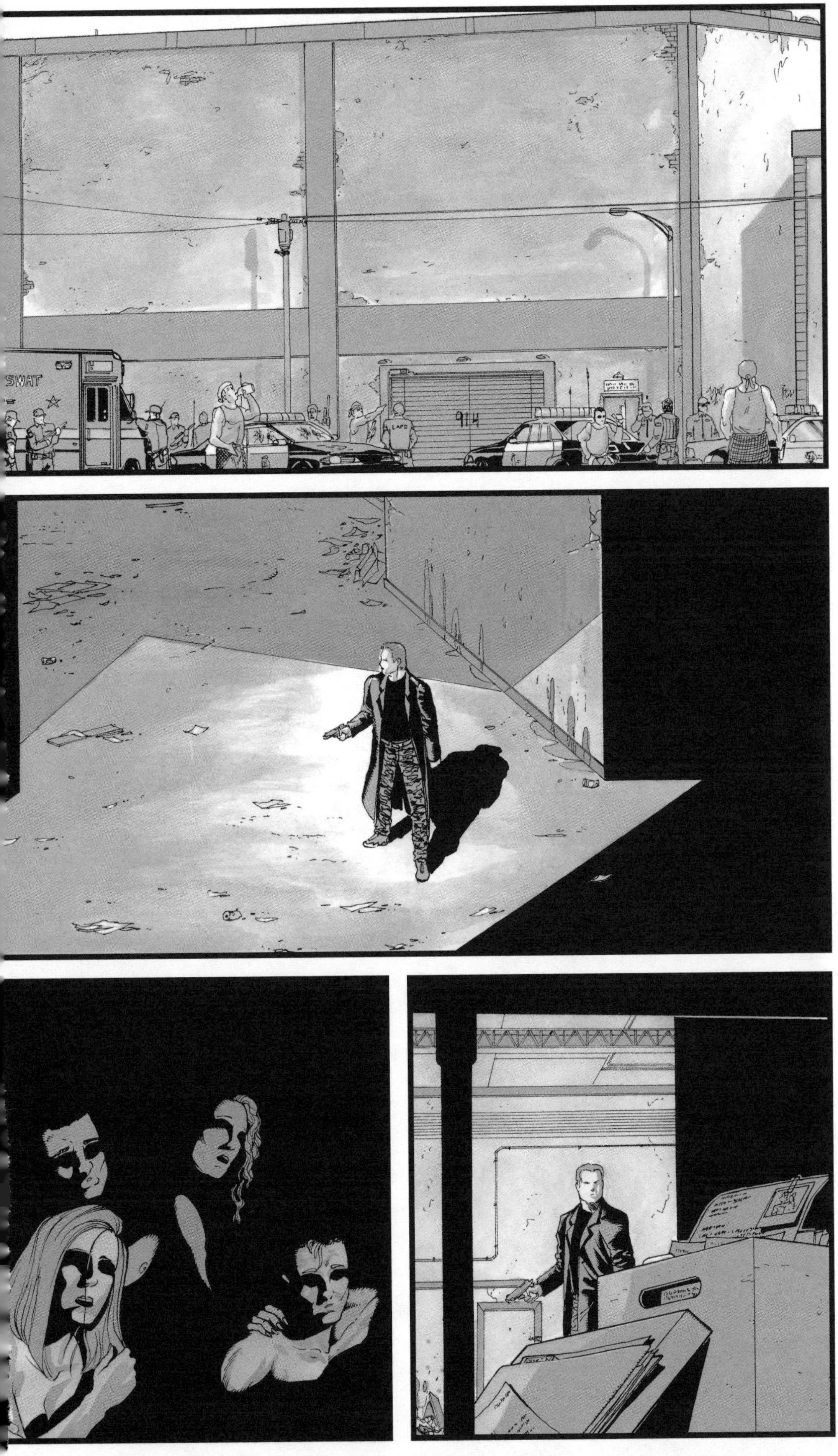
SWAT
LAPD
914

FUCK.

THEY WERE SO FUCKING SURE THEY WERE SAFE, THEY LEFT THE FUCKING PAPERWORK...

...ALL THE FUCKING RECEIPTS. UNREAL.

STANK LIKE AN AMATEUR JOB FROM THE START.

FUCKING EGOS WOULDN'T LET THEM NOT WRITE IT DOWN.

FUCK ME.

I SAW THIS BLOKE LAST FOUR FILMS.

AND SHE'S MARRIED TO HIM.

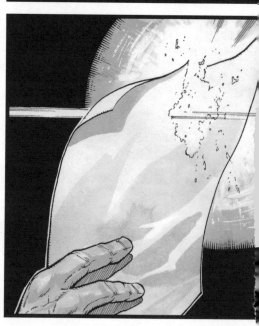

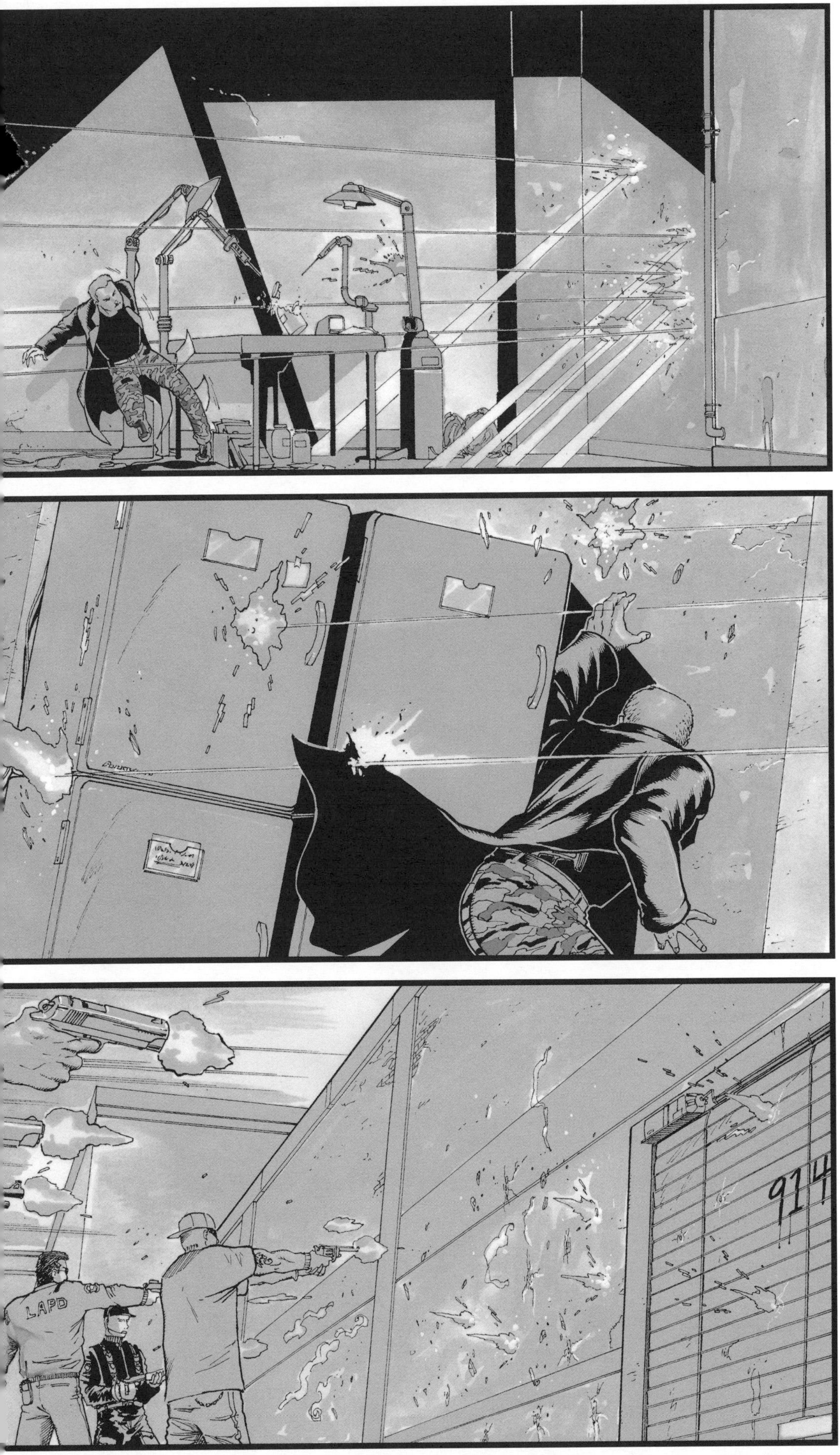
LAPD
914

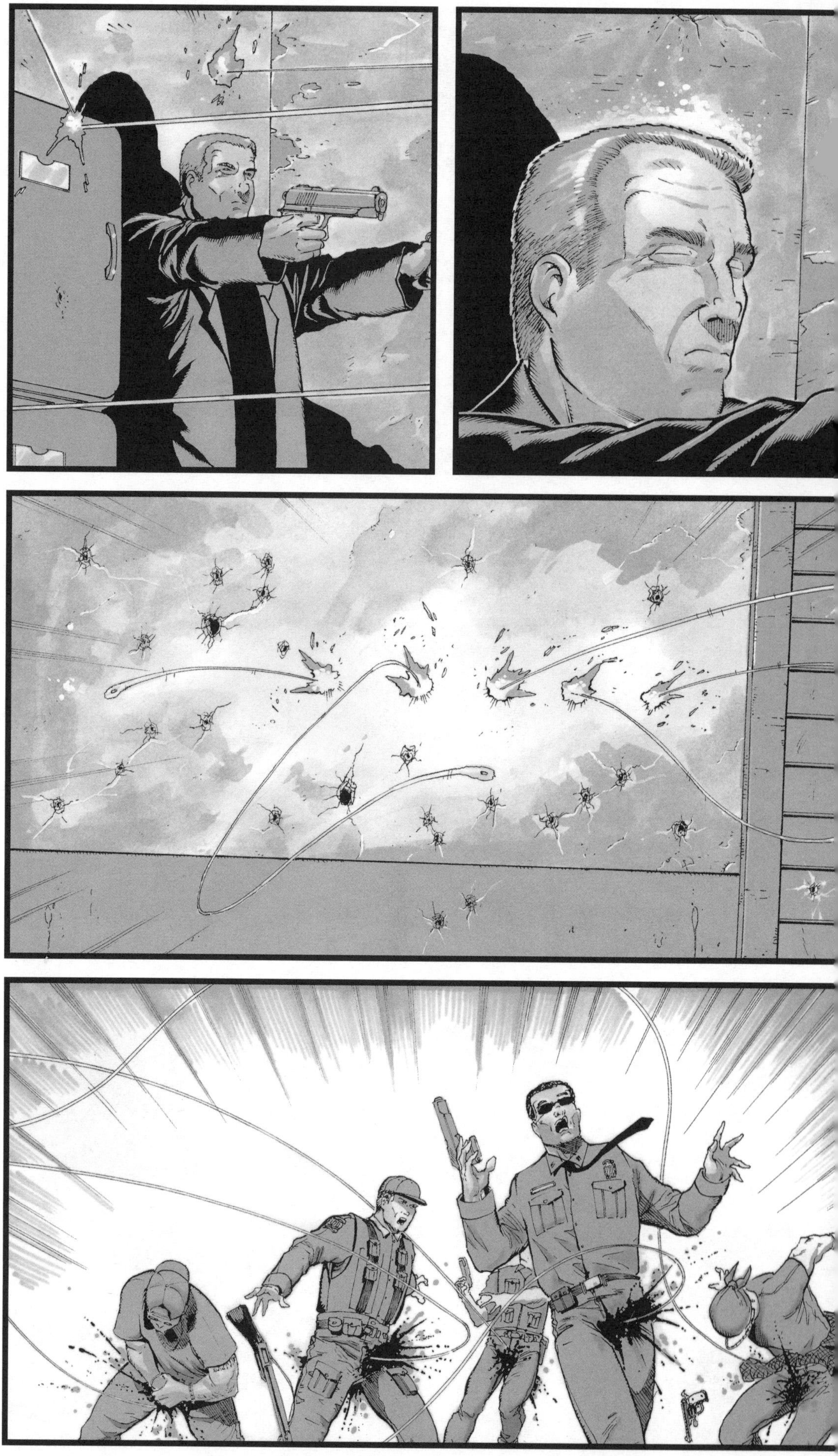

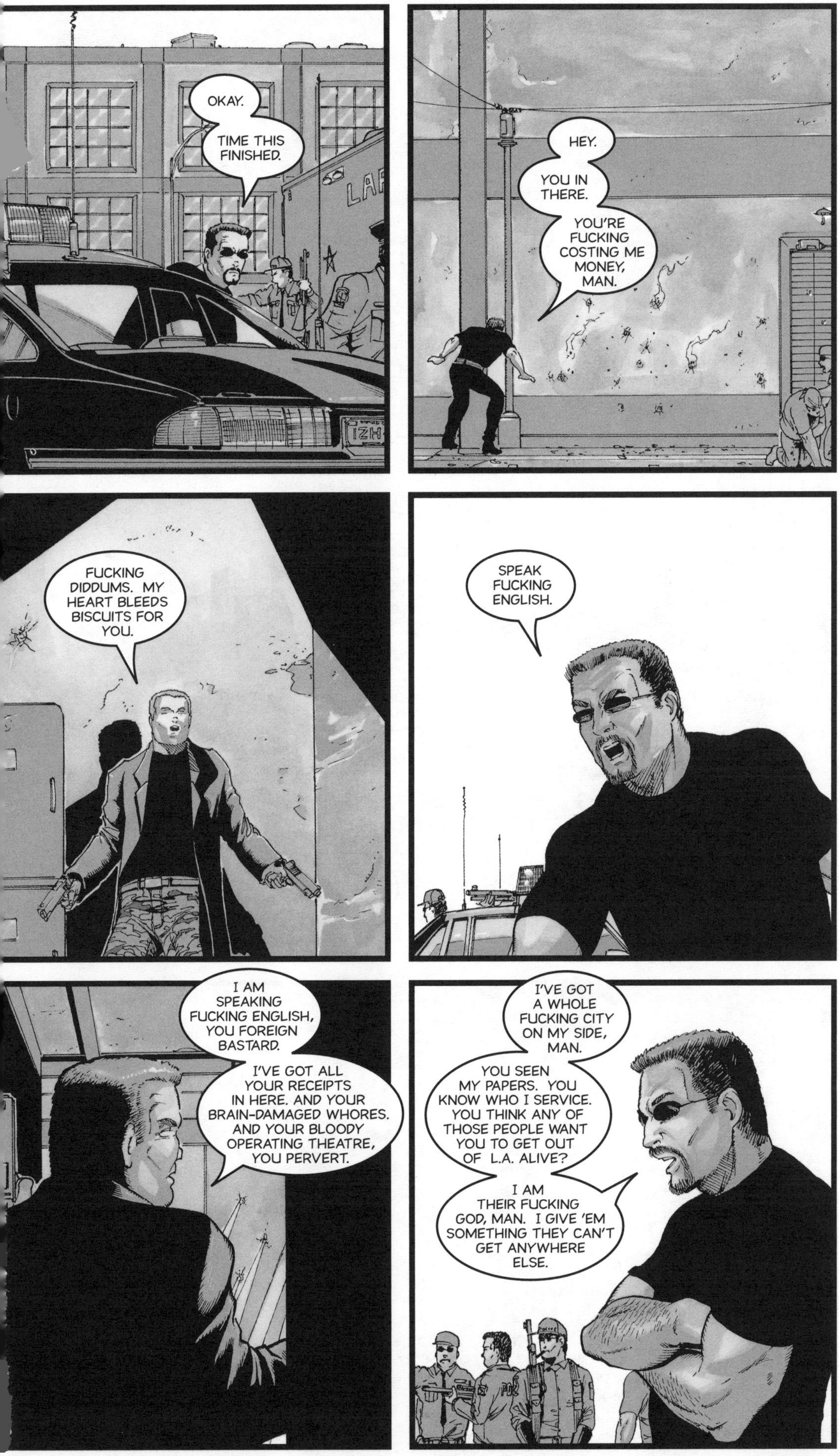
OKAY.
TIME THIS FINISHED.
HEY.
YOU IN THERE.
YOU'RE FUCKING COSTING ME MONEY, MAN.
FUCKING DIDDUMS. MY HEART BLEEDS BISCUITS FOR YOU.
SPEAK FUCKING ENGLISH.
I AM SPEAKING FUCKING ENGLISH, YOU FOREIGN BASTARD.
I'VE GOT ALL YOUR RECEIPTS IN HERE. AND YOUR BRAIN-DAMAGED WHORES. AND YOUR BLOODY OPERATING THEATRE, YOU PERVERT.
I'VE GOT A WHOLE FUCKING CITY ON MY SIDE, MAN.
YOU SEEN MY PAPERS. YOU KNOW WHO I SERVICE. YOU THINK ANY OF THOSE PEOPLE WANT YOU TO GET OUT OF L.A. ALIVE?
I AM THEIR FUCKING GOD, MAN. I GIVE 'EM SOMETHING THEY CAN'T GET ANYWHERE ELSE.

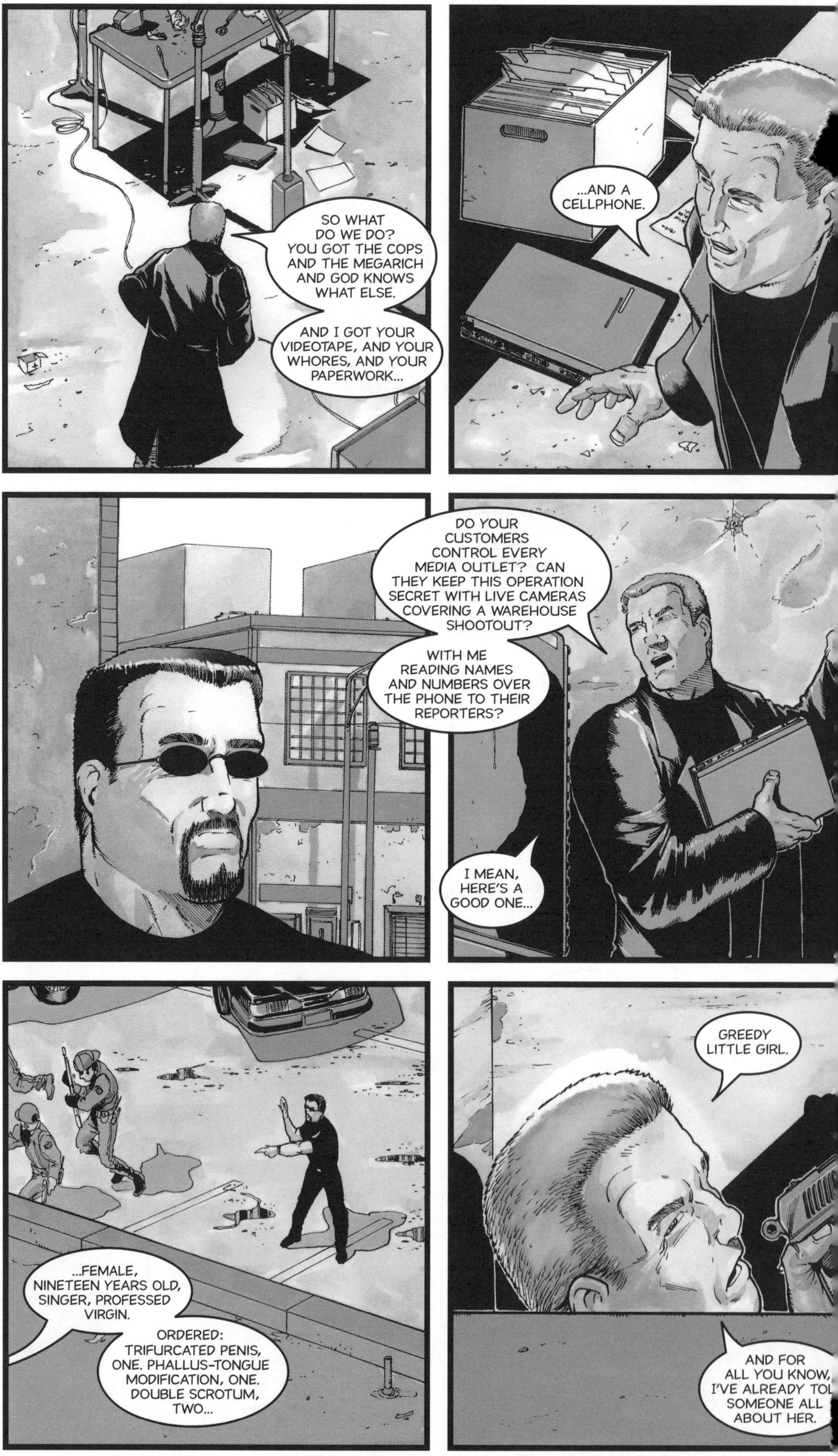
SO WHAT DO WE DO? YOU GOT THE COPS AND THE MEGARICH AND GOD KNOWS WHAT ELSE.
AND I GOT YOUR VIDEOTAPE, AND YOUR WHORES, AND YOUR PAPERWORK...
...AND A CELLPHONE.
DO YOUR CUSTOMERS CONTROL EVERY MEDIA OUTLET? CAN THEY KEEP THIS OPERATION SECRET WITH LIVE CAMERAS COVERING A WAREHOUSE SHOOTOUT?
WITH ME READING NAMES AND NUMBERS OVER THE PHONE TO THEIR REPORTERS?
I MEAN, HERE'S A GOOD ONE...
...FEMALE, NINETEEN YEARS OLD, SINGER, PROFESSED VIRGIN.
ORDERED: TRIFURCATED PENIS, ONE. PHALLUS-TONGUE MODIFICATION, ONE. DOUBLE SCROTUM, TWO...
GREEDY LITTLE GIRL.
AND FOR ALL YOU KNOW, I'VE ALREADY TOL SOMEONE ALL ABOUT HER.

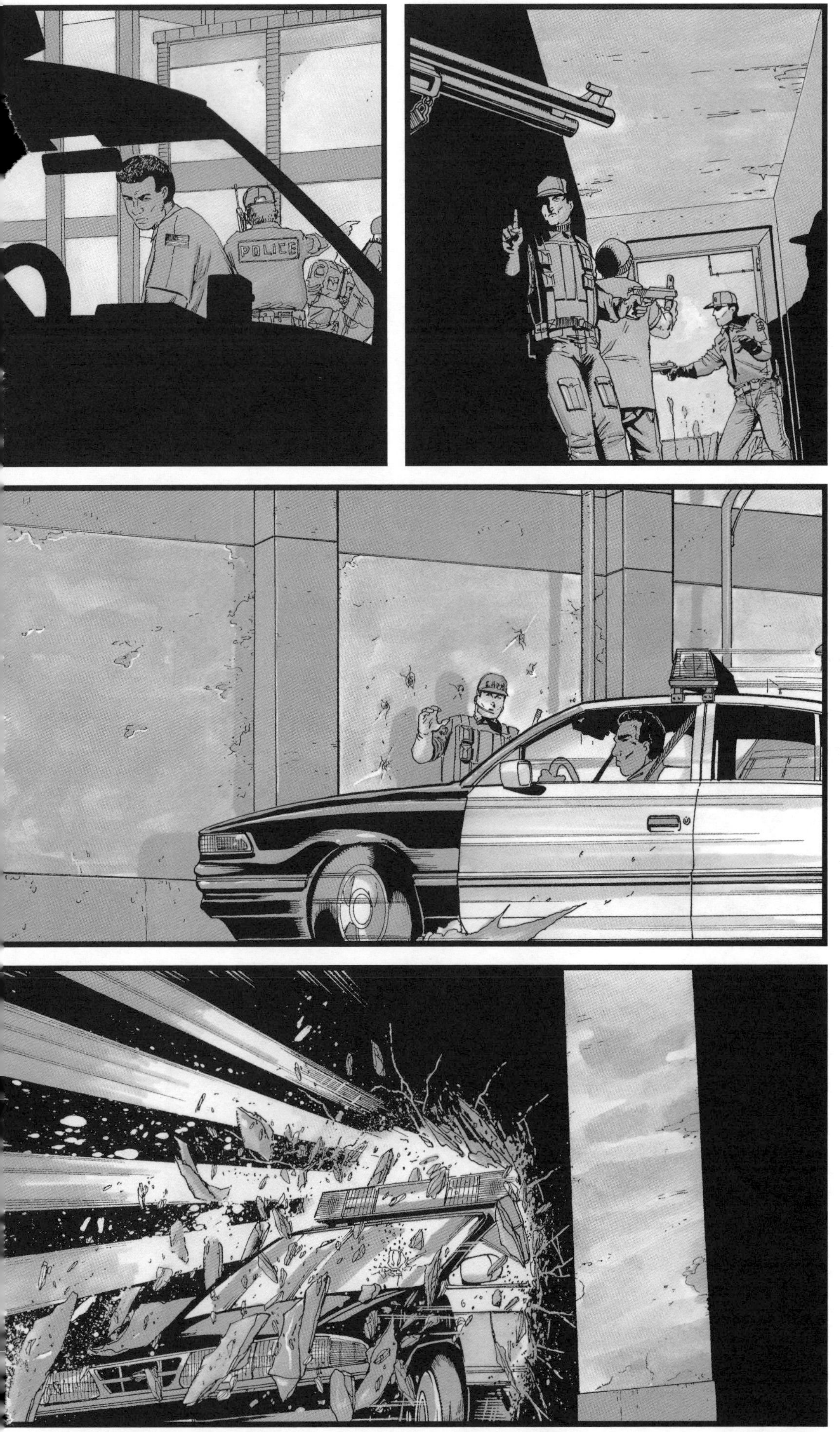
POLICE

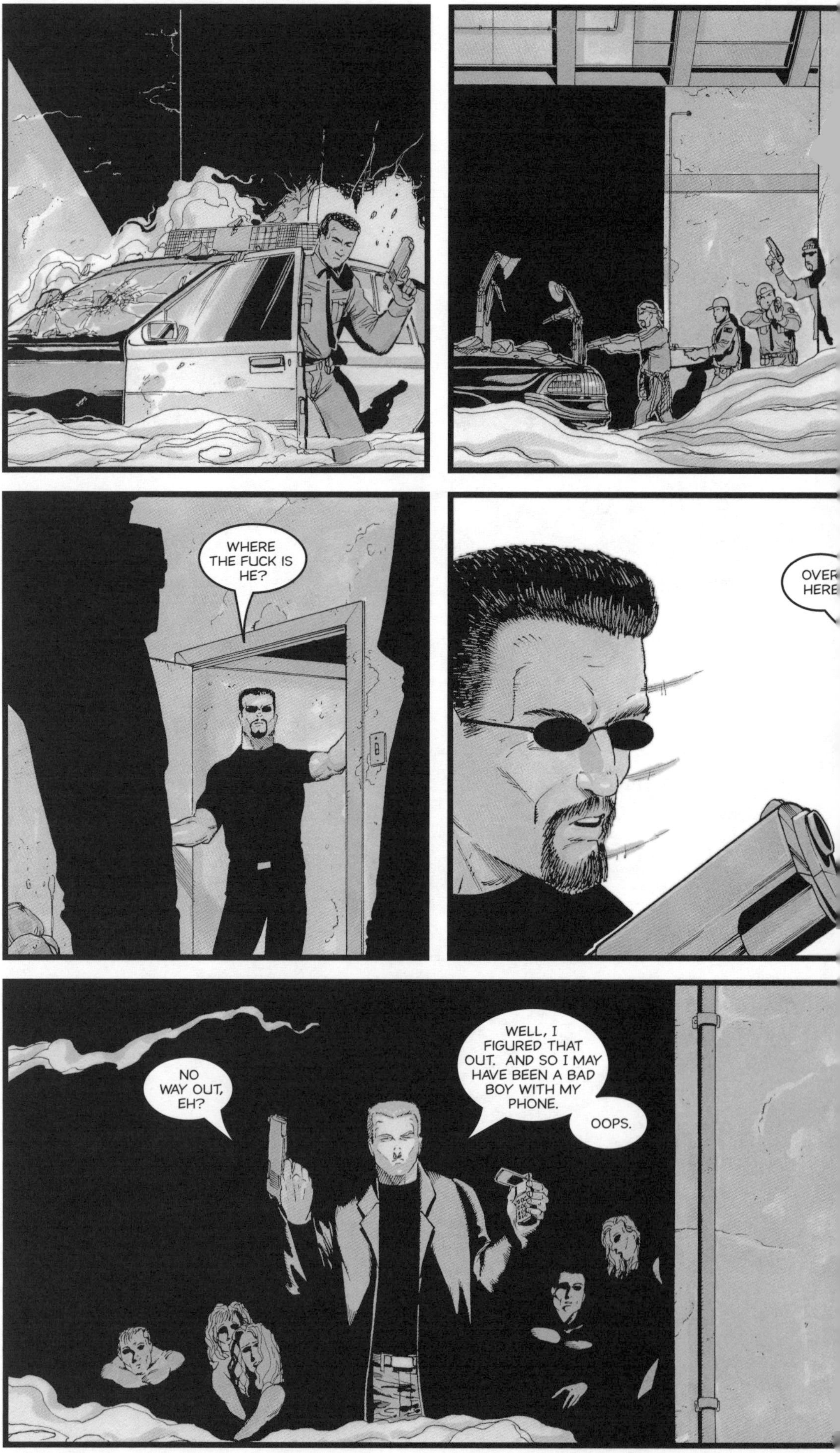
WHERE THE FUCK IS HE?
OVER HERE
NO WAY OUT, EH?
WELL, I FIGURED THAT OUT. AND SO I MAY HAVE BEEN A BAD BOY WITH MY PHONE.
OOPS.

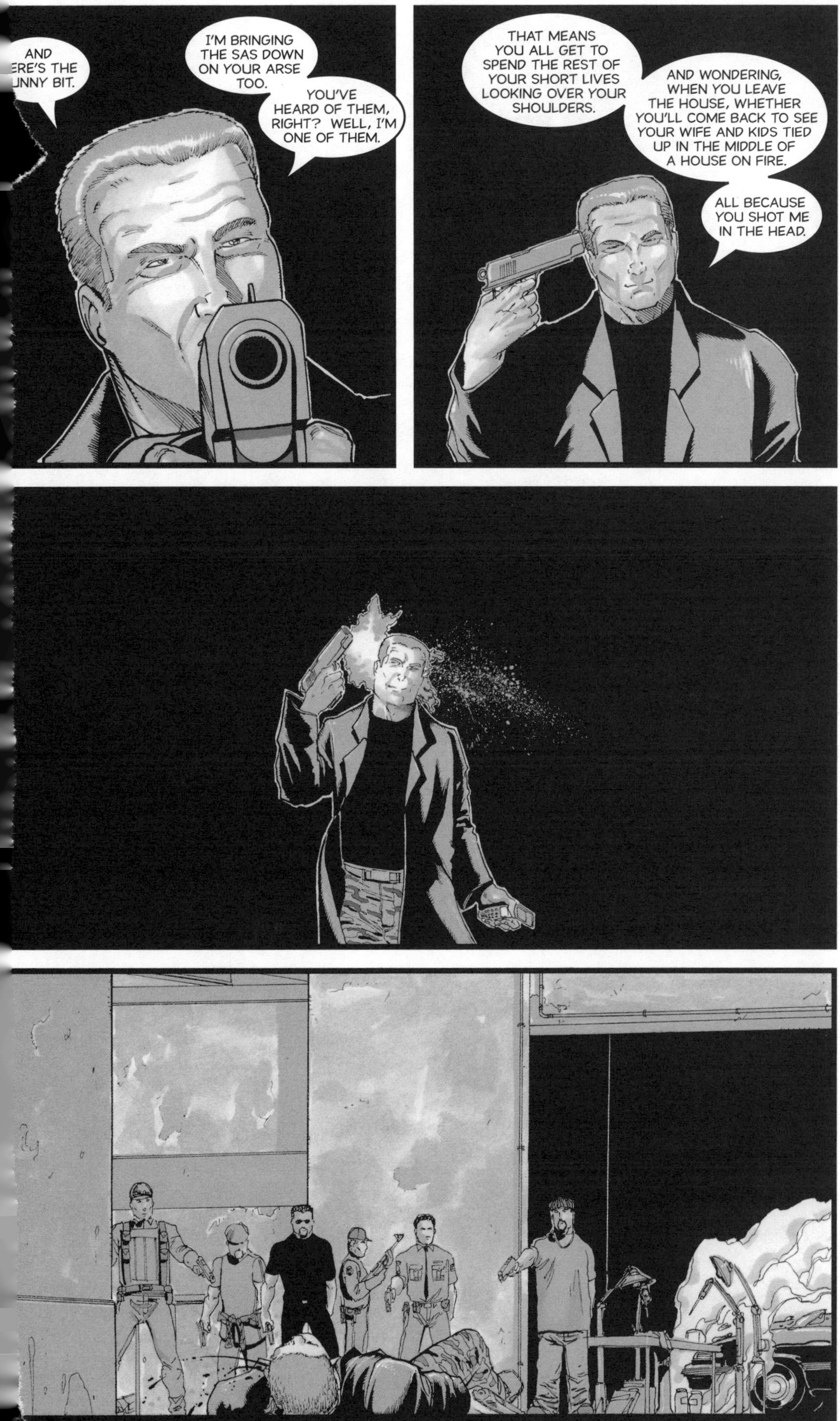
AND
ERE'S THE
UNNY BIT.
I'M BRINGING THE SAS DOWN ON YOUR ARSE TOO.
YOU'VE HEARD OF THEM, RIGHT? WELL, I'M ONE OF THEM.
THAT MEANS YOU ALL GET TO SPEND THE REST OF YOUR SHORT LIVES LOOKING OVER YOUR SHOULDERS.
AND WONDERING, WHEN YOU LEAVE THE HOUSE, WHETHER YOU'LL COME BACK TO SEE YOUR WIFE AND KIDS TIED UP IN THE MIDDLE OF A HOUSE ON FIRE.
ALL BECAUSE YOU SHOT ME IN THE HEAD.

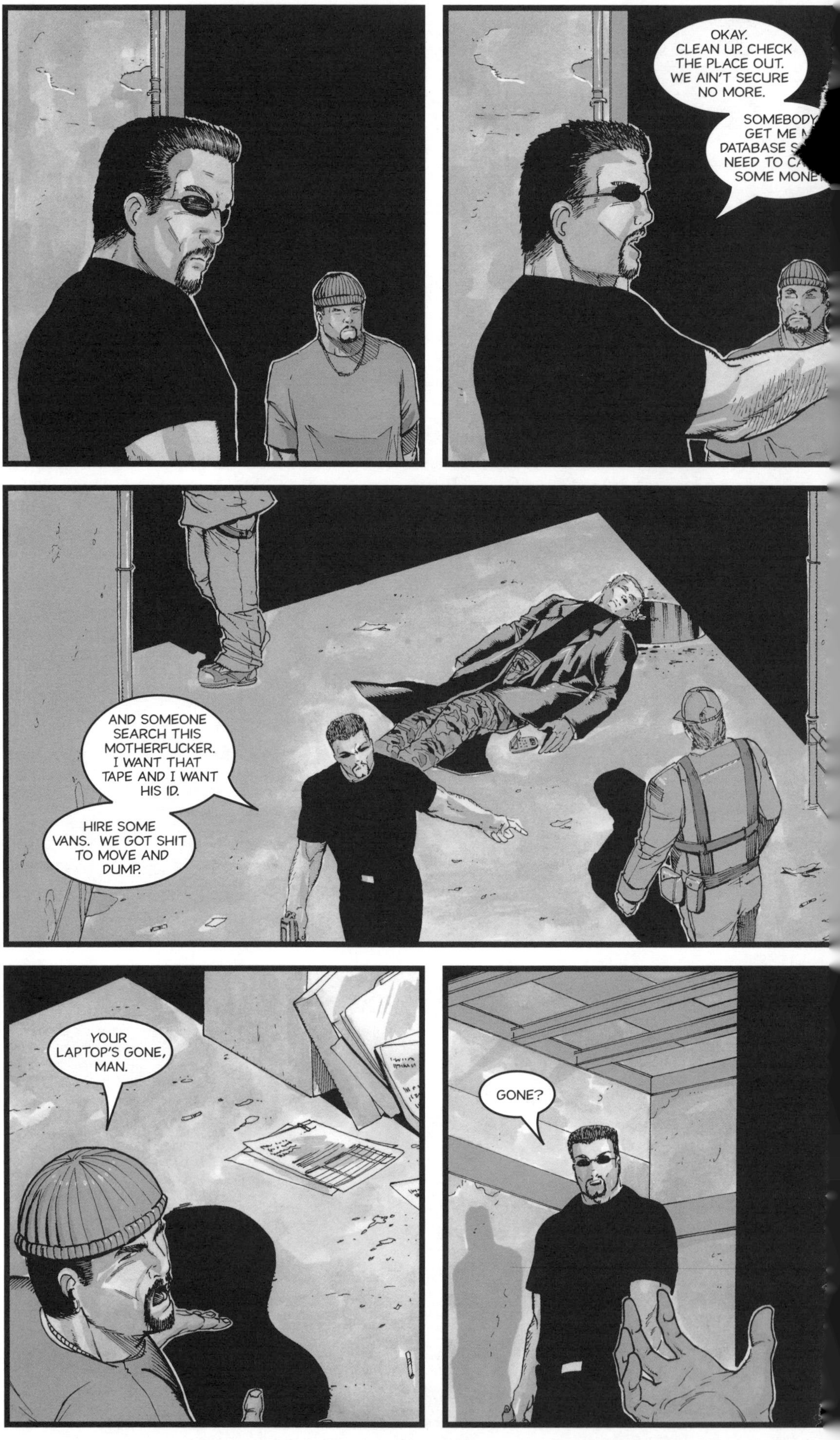
OKAY.
CLEAN UP. CHECK THE PLACE OUT. WE AIN'T SECURE NO MORE.
SOMEBODY GET ME M DATABASE S NEED TO CA SOME MONE
AND SOMEONE SEARCH THIS MOTHERFUCKER. I WANT THAT TAPE AND I WANT HIS ID.
HIRE SOME VANS. WE GOT SHIT TO MOVE AND DUMP.
YOUR LAPTOP'S GONE, MAN.
GONE?

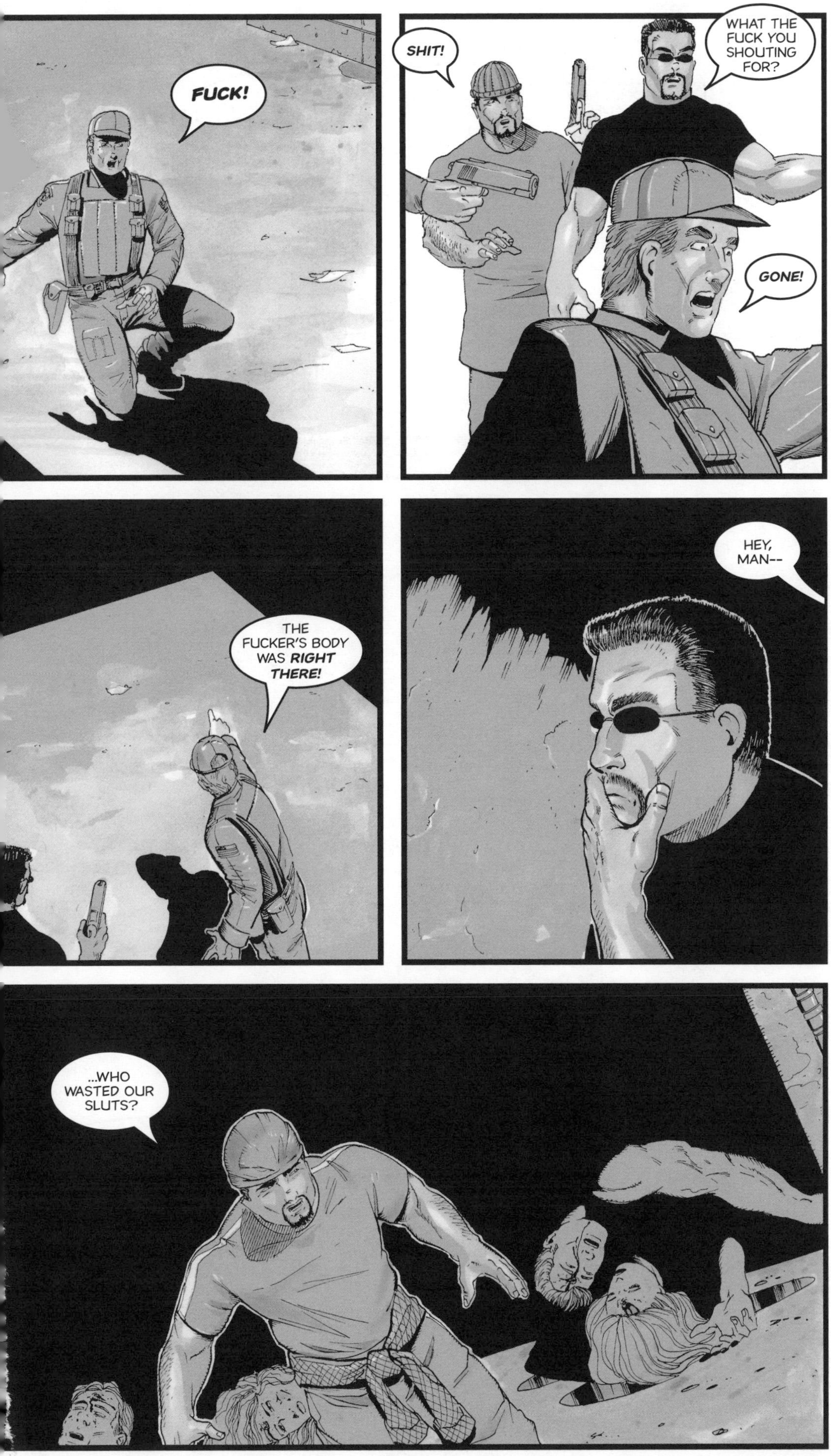
FUCK!
SHIT!
WHAT THE FUCK YOU SHOUTING FOR?
GONE!
THE FUCKER'S BODY WAS **RIGHT THERE!**
HEY, MAN--
...WHO WASTED OUR SLUTS?

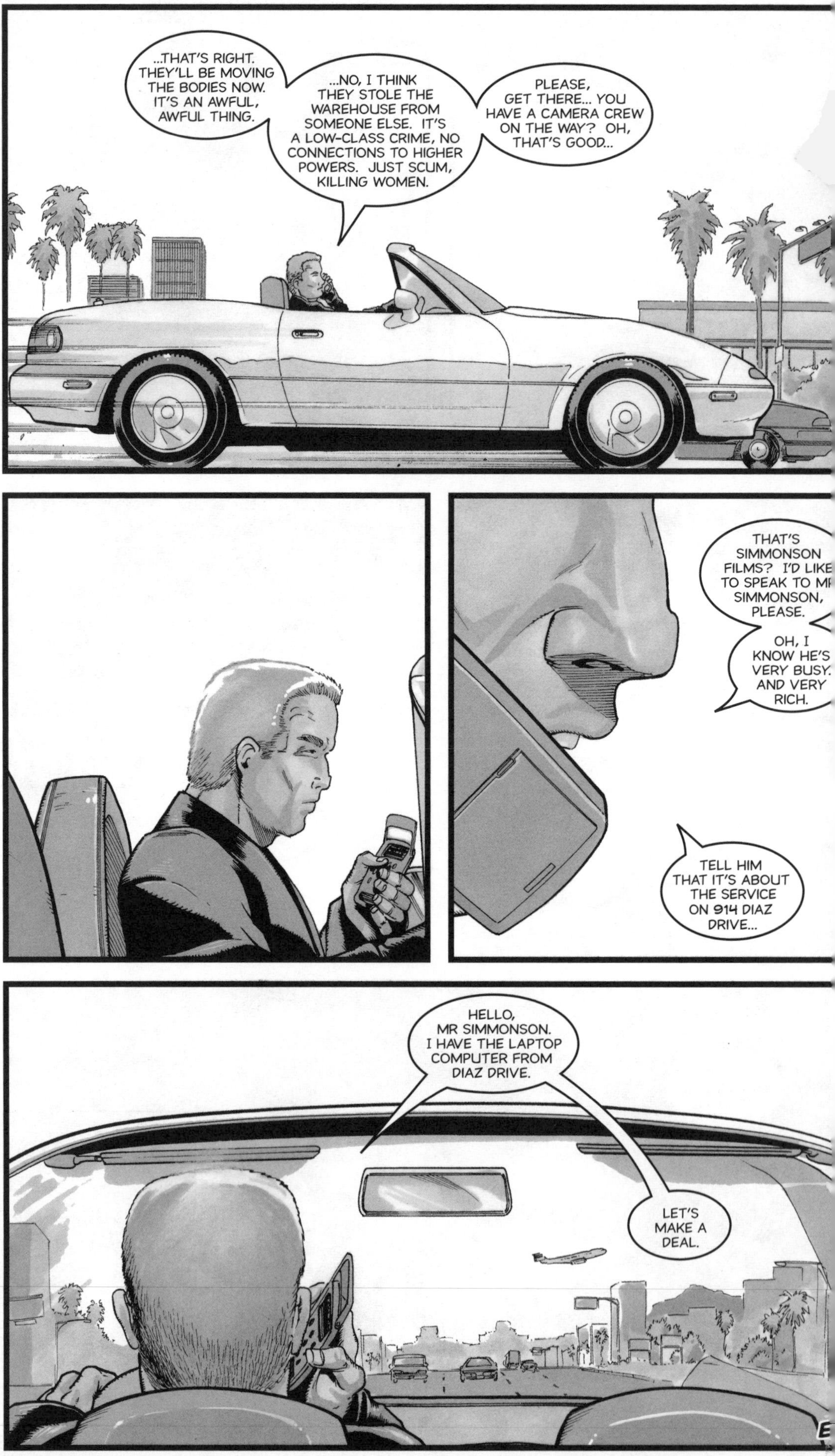
...THAT'S RIGHT. THEY'LL BE MOVING THE BODIES NOW. IT'S AN AWFUL, AWFUL THING.
...NO, I THINK THEY STOLE THE WAREHOUSE FROM SOMEONE ELSE. IT'S A LOW-CLASS CRIME, NO CONNECTIONS TO HIGHER POWERS. JUST SCUM, KILLING WOMEN.
PLEASE, GET THERE... YOU HAVE A CAMERA CREW ON THE WAY? OH, THAT'S GOOD...
THAT'S SIMMONSON FILMS? I'D LIKE TO SPEAK TO MR SIMMONSON, PLEASE.
OH, I KNOW HE'S VERY BUSY. AND VERY RICH.
TELL HIM THAT IT'S ABOUT THE SERVICE ON 914 DIAZ DRIVE...
HELLO, MR SIMMONSON. I HAVE THE LAPTOP COMPUTER FROM DIAZ DRIVE.
LET'S MAKE A DEAL.